The Volunteers

Cover design by Don Munson
Book design by Iris Bass

The Volunteers

MOACYR SCLIAR

Translated by
Eloah F. Giacomelli

AVAILABLE
PRESS

BALLANTINE BOOKS • NEW YORK

An Available Press Book
Published by Ballantine Books

Translation copyright © 1988 by Eloah F. Giacomelli

All rights reserved under International and Pan-American Copyright
Conventions. Published in the United States of America by Ballantine
Books, a division of Random House, Inc., New York, and simultaneously
in Canada by Random House of Canada Limited, Toronto. Originally
published in Portuguese as *Os Voluntarios* by L & PM Editores Ltda. in
1980. Copyright © 1980 by Moacyr Scliar.

Library of Congress Catalog Card Number: 88-91963

ISBN 0-345-35753-1

Manufactured in the United States of America

First Edition: September 1988

In memory of Sara Scliar,
who taught me how to tell stories.

For Judith and Roberto

Why be afraid of death? It is life's most beautiful adventure.

—Charles Frohman, a theatrical impresario, who sank with the *Lusitania* (May 7, 1915).

*By the rivers that flow
through Babylon I found myself*
—Camoëns

ON A DECEMBER NIGHT IN 1970, THE TUGBOAT *VOLUNTÁRIOS*
set sail from a wharf in Porto Alegre, its destination the port of
Haifa, in Israel. Its crew: four men (myself included) and a
woman. Its mission: to take a dying man to the legendary city
of Jerusalem.

I think now it can be told, the story of this voyage. The
people involved are no longer here; also, what else is there to
do in life besides telling stories? I, at least, do nothing else; I
spend my days here in the bar, leaning on the counter,
chewing the fat with my customers, and eating. I don't much
care for this line of business; I feel I'm growing apart from the
counter, partly because my belly gets bigger by the day, I
weigh well over one hundred kilos. My wife keeps nagging
me; she says she can no longer bear my weight, but it doesn't
bother me. I like this belly of mine. It's round, hairy; when
I'm in the bathtub, it surfaces from the whitish water as if it
were an island covered with underbrush. An island that no
navigator will ever come upon. It's not on any map. But then,
neither is Treasure Island. Do you know the story? A great
favorite of mine. As a matter of fact, I've always enjoyed

1

telling—and writing—stories. The teacher who taught us
Portuguese in school used to say that I had a knack for
storytelling; she always encouraged me to write—as she
encouraged other students, as well. She was a good teacher. She
died, pour soul. Luckily, before she ever saw me behind this
counter. As a matter of fact, I still follow her advice and read a
lot. National writers, foreign writers—I read everything, I'm
a fanatic for books, I enjoy reading so much that I can't help
mixing them in conversation.

But there's nothing I enjoy as much as telling stories. And
eating fried meat turnovers. The other day I polished off
eighteen of the forty my wife had made. She gets mad at me,
says she makes the meat turnovers to sell, not to feed me. It's
your own fault, I say to her, why do you have to make such
delicious meat turnovers? They're a specialty of hers. Not
exactly what Maria Amélia had hoped to accomplish in life;
her dream had been to become an opera singer. But she has
resigned herself to her fate; she realizes it's impossible
to have everything we want. Anyhow, she keeps singing while
she prepares the meat turnovers. Singing and arguing with
me. Full of fire, my wife is. I live between the frying pan
and the fire. That's a good one, isn't it? Between the frying
pan and the fire.

My wife is partly right, though, when she accuses me of not
looking after the business properly. We could remodel this
place, she keeps saying, change this old bar into a modern
luncheonette; look at those Vietnamese, they make a fortune
selling cheeseburgers with eggs, cheeseburgers without eggs.

I like the bar the way it is, the way I inherited it from my
father. But I must admit that she's right: we don't get many
customers, the place looks run-down. Take flies, for instance,
plenty of them around here. I've watched them so much that
I know them well. There's a big, bluish fly I find particularly
interesting. The mirror is her favorite hangout. She mistakes
her own reflected image for another fly, for a faithful companion
that follows her everywhere. I've named this ingenue Elvira.
There she is, see, over there? Come here, Elvira, come here!
She probably didn't hear me. Quite flighty, she is.

It was different in my father's time. The bar used to have a large patronage then; the mirror wasn't peeling as it is now. The premises were kept spotless; my father would frighten the flies away with an object that looked something like a whip—it was an emblem of African chieftaincy that he had brought from Mozambique, where he had served as an officer in the Portuguese colonial army. As a matter of fact, after taking part in the colonial war, he was so disgusted that he decided to leave Portugal. Newly wed, he came to Brazil. Instead of going to Rio, a city favored by his compatriots, he came to Porto Alegre.

My parents arrived here in 1935. They got off the ship on a stormy night, on a night when the river, enraged, was lashing against the stones of the wharf. They went to a hotel near the railroad station, an old hotel it was, with wooden partitions dividing the bedrooms. What with the rats scurrying in the attic above them, and the moanings, sighs, and giggles coming from the room adjoining theirs, they couldn't sleep. And on top of all that, the roof leaked; they had to keep moving the bed around all night long. This is awful, my mother kept saying, I want to sail back to Portugal first thing in the morning. My father remained silent. He wasn't a man who would go back on a decision. He was determined to stay in Brazil and to live here, not necessarily in luxury, but in easy circumstances.

At dawn the rain stopped and they went out for a walk in the Caminho Novo neighborhood. The last of the night people were leaving the cabarets, a drunk or two lay asleep in a doorway, women walked by yawning, tired, their makeup smudged, their dresses rumpled. That was what my mother saw, and what she saw displeased her.

It was with different eyes that my father watched this scene. Yes, he saw the drunks and the hookers. But he also saw a city waking up to face a day of work, a city eager for achievements and progress. My father saw the feverish hustle and bustle, the streetcars that kept arriving downtown, disgorging hundreds of hardworking Porto Alegre citizens: government employees carrying briefcases, bank clerks, young salesgirls hastening their steps, walking with their eyes fixed, their arms

folded against their chests. Hawkers were setting up their
wares; stores were opening their doors: dry-goods stores and
hardware stores, ready-to-wear stores and shoe stores; steel
doors were being rolled up; displayed in the show windows
were hoes and long johns, pea jackets and T-shirts, all thrown
up together in a haphazard way, but always at bargain prices;
mannequins with peeling noses smiled fixedly under their caps
and their *Ramenzoni* hats; yawning salesclerks were busy
placing remnants in hampers; on the frames of torn awnings,
merchants were hanging garish clothes, which kept flapping
in the morning breeze like, naturally, flags in the wind. Like
the banners that the Crusaders used to carry before them at
the time of the conquest of the Holy Land. What Father failed
to notice, however, was the poor quality of those clothes,
made from inferior wool. He didn't know then that it was wool
woven from the fleece of stolen sheep, certainly the worst
possible sheep, the kind that vultures, trained by sly hunters,
could snatch up and transport through the air—an ingenious
trick devised by thieves, something my father would never have
imagined if the hawker Peep-Less, a former frontiersman,
had not told him about it years later. (But, one might wonder,
wasn't the whole story just a figment of Peep-Less's
imagination?)

My father saw not only modest little stores, but also buildings
still displaying their past grandeur. He saw façades ornamented
with festoons and stone figures, buildings with castlelike turrets.
In the light of that dawn, here on Rua Voluntários da Pátria,
on this street named after the Volunteers of the Fatherland, my
father sensed a strange, mystical atmosphere. While on the one
hand the headlights of an old Model-A Ford struck him as
being the eyes of a prehistoric monster (and many a prehistoric
monster had haunted the dreams of my father, especially in
Mozambique), on the other hand, the cafe whose doors the fat,
smiling proprietor was just then opening looked inviting, and
the aroma of freshly brewed coffee and of freshly baked rolls
emanating from the inside reminded him of his childhood.
The show windows of the hardware stores displayed sturdy,
good-quality tools, just what a person needed to earn an

honest living; and in the owners of the grocery stores, my father
recognized his compatriots. He decided he would set up shop
somewhere in this area as a restaurateur or bar owner. And so,
with his savings, he bought this Lusitania Bar, where I still
work behind the counter.

When Father acquired the bar, I hadn't been born yet. The
invisible particles that would later make up my bones, my
hairs, my fluids, still lay scattered throughout nature's kingdom.
But it so happened that an ant from this state of Rio Grande
do Sul dropped a speck of Rio Grande do Sul soil onto a leaf of
kale—grown, naturally, in Rio Grande do Sul—and my
mother was to eat this kale. A sardine was caught somewhere
in the Brazilian territorial waters, and my father was to eat
this sardine. And an egg was laid by a certain hen and, well ...
what I want to say is that by that time I was already closer to
Brazil, to Rio Grande do Sul, to Rua Voluntários, than I was to
my ancestors. I was already not far away from this counter in
the Lusitania Bar.

My father was happy here. He enjoyed cooking, which he
would do with dignity, wielding the skimmer as if it were a
royal scepter. Although he was from a poor family, his ancestors
included two baronets, several knights-errant, and at least one
Crusader: Sisenando, the Mute, whose tongue had been cut off
by the Saracens. With gestures, this fierce man would convey
his greatest wish in life, which was to knock down the walls of
Jerusalem: fist upon fist—the walls; head striking the fists—a
ramming rod knocking down the walls; a finger on the
neck—the execution of the Saracens. Sisenando, the Mute, died
without having fulfilled his dream of beheading thousands of
infidels.

Valiant ancestors. They would have enjoyed taking part in
our adventure. They would have used a different strategy,
surely, like besieging their enemy for a long period of time
before assailing their walls. It's unlikely that temerity was
their forte. But even so, I've always admired them. And I must
say that their spirits were with me when we set off on our
voyage.

My father was a tall, elegant man. Nothing like those

bald-headed, mustachioed Portuguese in T-shirts depicted in
caricatures. Father had a beautiful head of hair; he wore his
mustache carefully trimmed. He always wore a dark suit, gold
cuff links, and a pearl pin on his necktie. Dressed up like that,
mind you, here in the bar, whose customers weren't exactly
counts or barons, just merchants from the neighborhood, as well
as hawkers, taxi drivers, and blue-collar workers. Standing
behind the cash register (huge it was, made of silver-plated,
filigreed metal), he would formally greet the customers as
they walked in.

Although it wasn't a big commercial establishment, it had
some sophisticated touches: gilt-edged mirrors, plaster molding
around the ceiling, ceiling fans with big blades that kept
rotating slowly. The counter and the tables were marble-
topped. On the wall at the back, a mural: caravels on a billowy
sea, and the name of the house: LUSITANIA BAR-RESTAURANTE.

Father's friends couldn't understand why he had set up shop
on Rua Voluntários, a street of wholesale businesses and small
stores, peopled with hawkers, hookers, and con artists. A man
like him, they would say, should have opened a pastry shop
on Rua da Praia, or a teahouse on Rua Independência.

Or a men's clothing store, like the ones on Rua da Praia; or a
stylish shoe store; or a small, elegant, unobtrusive, watchmaker's
shop. They would have approved of a hardware store, with a
diversified stock of useful tools and a staff of diligent
salesclerks—young men looking like farmhands or old men in
blue denim aprons, with eyeglasses pushed back over their
foreheads, a pencil stuck behind their ears. Or my father could
have owned an electric supplies store, like the ones on Rua
Alberto Bins, with their small chalkboards on which the
proprietors announced that the valves with the listed code
numbers were now in stock. Or a chinaware store: coffeepots,
sugar bowls, coffee and dinnerware sets. Or a haberdashery,
like the ones on Rua Floresta—small, gloomy establishments
where shoppers were attended to by overweight matrons and
bald-headed gentlemen wearing gold-rimmed eyeglasses and
gray sweaters, their mouths drooping at the corners. Or even
a furniture store, like the ones in Bom Fim, would have been

acceptable: an old, long building, crammed with yellow pine
wardrobes and beds, with the distrustful proprietor and his
assistant (usually a tubercular-looking mulatto who lived in
the district of Partenon), lurking in the back. Or why not a
confectionery with some Germanic name, its showcases
displaying cheesecakes and pastries? Or a specialty store carrying
imported products—Spanish wines, Norwegian anchovies,
Danish cheeses, delicacies from all over the world?

But no, my father had chosen Rua Voluntários. Was it a
secret fascination for the grotesque caused by an inordinate
contemplation of African masks, or was it caused by a curse cast
upon him by the tribal witch doctors? Hard to tell. The fact
is that my father remained on Rua Voluntários. Without losing,
as he himself used to say, his aplomb. Always a well-
mannered man, even with the hookers, whom he addressed as
senhora and *ma'am*. A gentleman who appreciated fine wines
and good literature. It was he who introduced me to the works
of the nineteenth-century Portuguese writer Herculano, for
instance. True, later I came to prefer the books in the popular
Terramarear Collection, *Treasure Island* being my favorite; but
it wasn't for lack of encouragement on the part of my father. I
was only a little boy when I was first exposed to the poetry of
Camoëns, the great sixteenth-century Portuguese poet. Father
would recite his poems to me (the way other fathers would
narrate stories to their children): *By the rivers that flow through
Babylon / I found myself . . .* A really cultivated man, my
father was. He also appreciated good theater; he wasn't rich—
we've never been rich, quite the opposite—but whenever
there was a performance at the Coliseu or at the São Pedro
Theater, he'd be there, up in the gallery, where the seats were
cheaper. By himself; Mother didn't care for such things.

My mother was a small, thin woman. Decorously dressed,
almost always in black because of the many deaths in her
family. She hardly ever smiled. Not that she was an irascible
woman, but she was afflicted by some kind of melancholy
that made her heave a sigh every once in a while, quite audible
over the sizzling of the frying pan in which, at home, she
would fry codfish balls, which my father would take to the

Lusitania Bar-Restaurante; they were the specialty of the
house. Poor Mother. She died, poor soul. Of tuberculosis. A
disease that ran in her family.

My father outlived her by a few years. In his last years,
however, he let things slide; he stopped wearing neckties, his
jacket had grease stains on it. The flies would walk on his
forehead. His face was afflicted with some kind of eczema,
which made him look even more pitiful. Finally he, too, died.

From my childhood I've nothing but good memories. We
used to live on Rua Comendador Coruja, in a house that
even in those days was already old. I can still vividly recall its
front door, made of solid wood, with a hand-shaped knocker;
it was this hand, with its solid fingers knocking on a metal
disk, that let the family—a small family, for I was an only
child—know that an outsider wanted to see us. I remember the
windows with their etched panes, and the lace curtains, which
my mother had made, depicting biblical scenes: Isaac's sacrifice,
Jacob courting Rachel, Solomon and the Queen of Sheba.
Those were the curtains in the front room, which was a
spacious parlor. In the bedrooms and in the dinette, the
curtains depicted young shepherdesses tending sheep. I remember
the front door, with the three marble steps already quite
worn out; the floor, with its creaking boards; the attic, crisscrossed
at night by galloping mice and the ghosts of my childhood
days—the specter of Sisenando, the Mute, being one of the least
frightening; many a sabbat had the witches held in that attic,
many a beheaded body had roamed there in search of its head.
For a period of time the backyard of our house was the sea
where I would sail in a boat made of crates, the battlefield
where, together with brave barons, I would confront the
Moors of the Holy Land. A good backyard it was, with lush
grass, shade trees, and stones that marked hiding places and
secret tunnels. That backyard was big enough to hold me in for
a long time—until an irresistible impulse finally hurled me
out into the streets, and from then on, the streets were all I
wanted. Rua Voluntários, the docks, the railroad station, the
market, that's where I hung out. I knew by name the boatmen
that brought oranges from the town of Taquari to the fruit

dock, the railroad engineers, the truckers who drove their
trunks from the interior. I was particularly fond of the
hawker Peep-Less, who was then a young man newly arrived
from the interior. He was a gaucho from Alegrete, a town
near the Argentinian border, but a different sort of gaucho:
where you expected fierce eyes and a huge mustache, you
found small, melancholy eyes and a thin mustache; where you
visualized broad shoulders and sinewy arms, there were
stooping shoulders and puny arms. Peep-Less had grown up on
a cattle ranch. He left for the big city after losing his wife to
tuberculosis and his young son to diarrhea. Himself a former
TB sufferer, he had one thing to be proud of: his voice—
twangy, metallic, surprisingly strong. At one time he had
considered becoming a country music singer, but not your
run-of-the-mill singer; what he had in mind was to combine
hillbilly music and gaucho songs with demonstrations of lasso
wielding. After being disqualified in an amateur singers program
of the Farroupilha Radio, he became a hawker, using his
voice—the only good thing about me, he'd say—to advertise the
curative properties of the Capema Herbal Elixir, a wonder
recommended for a thousand different problems: bladder stones,
varicose veins, asthma, depression, poor memory, fallen uterus,
ovarian inflammation. Leaving his boardinghouse in the Lower
City quite early in the morning, he would arrive at his usual
spot on Rua Voluntários, not far from Praça Parobé, at the time
when the buses began to unload dozens of passengers in the
bus station—newcomers arriving, as he himself had once arrived,
from the interior of the state, dazed from the journey,
astounded and alarmed at the sight of the tall buildings, the
streetcars, the automobiles. Carrying their bundles of clothes
and their cardboard suitcases, they would walk on aimlessly,
swept along by the crowds already swelling on Rua Voluntários.
Meanwhile, Peep-Less would be setting up his little table, on
which he would then place the flasks of his elixir before taking
his helpers—Catarina the Snake, the Pascoal the Lizard—out
of a small suitcase.

Like their owner, the Snake and the Lizard came from the
country, from the frontier. Quite old, they were: Peep-Less

had gotten them from his predecessor, a hawker who had been a friend of his father's. Under the amazed, or frightened, or amused eyes of the bystanders, the reptiles would lie motionless on the top of the small suitcase while Peep-Less cried his wares. "Why be in pain?" he would shout. "Kill your pains, and smile again."

All gung ho in the morning, he would gradually lose his pep as the day progressed. By late afternoon he had shouted himself hoarse, the voice he was so proud of barely audible. He would then put his reptiles in the small suitcase, pack the flasks of elixir, fold the little table, and come over to the Lusitania for a drink. In those hours he was smitten with sudden melancholy, with devastating homesickness. Birds far from their nests peep less, he would then say, an expression that earned him his nickname. Opening his jacket, he would take some money out of his leather money belt to pay for his drink. That beautifully crafted money belt with a silver buckle was his only keepsake of the cattle ranch. Upon arriving in Porto Alegre, he sold his gaucho paraphernalia: his *bombachas,* the long, accordion-pleated trousers, closely fitting around the waist and ankles, worn by the cowboys of Rio Grande do Sul; the boots and spurs that he used to wear on feast days; and even his maté *cuia,* the small, silver-rimmed bottle gourd and his *bomba,* the silver tube with a strainer on the end through which the gauchos sip *chimarrao,* the green unsweetened maté.

A sorrowful man. Only once did I see him happy. He had been crying out the wonders of his elixir to a small crowd when all of a sudden a horse appeared right in the middle of Rua Voluntários. An old horse, bridleless, it must have run away from a drayman; halting in front of Peep-Less, it stood there, motionless.

The eyes of the hawker glittered.

Setting aside the flasks of elixir, Catarina the Snake, and Pascoal the Lizard, he made his way—"excuse me, excuse me"—toward the old bay. Gingerly he put out his hand to stroke the horse's muzzle and neck. Suddenly, in one leap, he mounted the animal. The horse stood still. With the heel of his shoes, Peep-Less spurred it on, then, with the hawker holding

on to its mane, the horse broke into a gentle trot along Rua
Voluntários, in the direction of the city center. The incident
almost ended in tragedy: all excited, Peep-Less began to ride at
a gallop down the street—"out of my way, folks!"—and as he
was approaching the intersection, he bumped into a streetcar
that was just then turning the corner. The horse was knocked
down by the impact; Peep-Less, thrown off the horse, was lucky
he wasn't hurt. Limping, he walked up to the dying animal,
took a look at him, then came here to borrow my father's
revolver and, with one shot, put an end to the animal's
suffering. Later he had to indemnify the outraged drayman for
the loss of his horse. But it was worth every cent, he would
say. To gallop that horse, it was well worth it.

A deeply religious man, a real ascetic, every year Peep-Less
would take part in the reenactment of the Passion of Christ,
held on the Hill of the Cross. Wearing only a loincloth and a
crown of thorns, he would carry a heavy cross on his
shoulders. He would do this so that the souls of his wife and
son could rest in peace. On such occasions, he became
transfigured: he felt that he was really Christ. It's as if I
were in Jerusalem, Paulo, he said to me once, and that was the
first time anybody had ever talked to me, talked to me in
real earnest, that is, about Jerusalem; and long before
Benjamin.

Peep-Less was my friend, but by no means the only one. I
hung out with a crowd, and a large crowd it was, of kids
roughly my own age—nine, ten, twelve years old: kids from
Rua Floresta, from Rua Comendador Coruja, and even from
Rua Voluntários. Our fathers were merchants. We attended
the elementary schools of the neighborhood; after class we got
together and then time never hung heavy on our hands. We
played marble games, a matter of life and death; improvising a
ball with socks, we played fierce soccer games; and we
collected things, such as the hard-to-get picture stamps that
came with the *Carlitos* and *Brocoió* candies, postage stamps,
old Brazilian coins. Following a well-devised route, we scouted

about the city streets in search of empty cigarette packs.
Leaving Rua Voluntários, which offered nothing but empty
packs of the ordinary brands (*Liberty*, *Baliza*, *Colomy*, *Tu-
Fuma*, *Caporal*, *Douradinho*), we would turn into Rua Floresta
(*Hollywood*, *Continental*, things began to look up there), and
head for Moinhos de Ventos, a neighborhood full of mansions,
where we always had a good chance of coming upon a rare
brand with gold lettering against a red background: *Odalisca*!
Did we know what an odalisque was? Vaguely. That it
referred to a woman, we knew; that she must be gorgeous, we
conjectured; but we never even suspected that she lived in a
harem, that she wore a veil and enveloped herself in gauze, that
she was the property of the sultan, but even if we had known
about such things, they wouldn't have made any difference; we
wouldn't have loved her less. We might, however, have
considered leading a war against the sultan's troops, that's for
sure.

We were experienced in wars and guerrilla warfare. Often, in
the course of our expeditions across the city, we would enter
unknown territory; and then, from somewhere—from a treetop,
a balcony, a rooftop, or from behind a dilapidated wall—
would come a hail of stones. The enemy!

Disbanding immediately, we would run for shelter. We
would draw our weapons: our dependable slingshots. Mine
was a forked stick from a guava tree, and the strap was red
rubber, the best kind available. For missiles I kept pebbles
from the riverbank in a pouch hanging from my neck (but
some of the other kids, including one who is nowadays a
member of the Chamber of Deputies, used steel pellets).

Sometimes the enemy forces were superior to ours. In that
case we didn't think it shameful to flee. We fled, we sought
refuge. If, however, there were only six or so sharpshooters, we
would beleaguer them. The siege of the enemy fortress—a
vacant lot, an abandoned house—could last for hours, but it
always culminated in a final attack, and then it was anything
goes: punches, kicks, hammerlocks, blows delivered with a stick,
and even—but only very rarely, for we weren't bandits—
knives and switchblades. There were also some exotic weapons.
There was a kid in our group who always fought with a

short chain with thick links; another one wore brass knuckles,
which he had bought from a sailor. But we weren't bandits;
no, we weren't.

(We were not bandits, or were we? Peep-Less thought we
were. Bandits, that's what you are, he would often shout at
us, in a rage. Even though we were his friends, we couldn't
help making fun of him, and we would mimic the way he
cried out his wares. Once we tried to steal his snake; furious, he
drew a switchblade on us: Don't you dare touch Catarina, not
Catarina, you bandits!)

On Sundays the warriors rested. We never fought on Sundays,
we never shed blood on the Lord's Day. On Sundays we went
to the movies: at the Coliseu, near my father's bar, or at the
Apolo, farther away, on Rua Independência. That was the age
of the movie serials. Together with Flash Gordon we flew to
distant planets; together with Nyoka we faced indescribable
dangers. We waged war against Indians from various nations,
the Cheyennes being particularly fearful; we fought in the
Foreign Legion, we were attacked by snakes and tigers, by
octopuses and bats. In short, we lived moments fraught with
tension. Gradually the hot, stuffy movie theater became
impregnated with our miasmas and with the smoke from the
cigarettes that we smoked on the sly, lest the manager kick
us out.

We had devised a code system for ourselves. At the word
mandrake, we froze still. We spoke pig Latin. We kept track
of car plate numbers, and starting with a number ending in zero,
we tried to work our way up to one hundred. Sometimes we
came pretty close to reaching this goal—but then we happened
to see a bespectacled black man on the street and we had to
start all over again. We entered into secret pacts signed with
blood obtained by pricking the tip of a finger with a pin,
which was almost never sterilized; we had a thousand different
shelters and hideouts, which we used mainly to hide from the
girls. They, too, pretended to ignore us as they played ring-
around-a-rosy: *By lifting a stone/Then what, what, what*. We
had no use for such children's games. We had other dreams,
other aspirations: adventure, that's what we were after. From

the riverbank we would gaze at the islands, to us still remote, still mysterious. We supposed there were pirates and cannibals there, as well as castles hidden amid the vegetation, and treasures buried under the roots of the trees. But how to get there? By swimming? We lacked the stamina to do so. What we needed was a boat.

This boat—a sailboat, a motorboat, an old ship, anything— this boat was my dream. I would imagine myself sailing down the Guaiba River, past the town of Itapuã, then across the lake, until I reached the sea, and finally, Africa. Only in dreams: a boat was a forbidden thing. My father, usually rather tolerant, was adamant about it. This river is very treacherous, he would argue, and indeed, it wasn't unusual for corpses to be seen floating on its muddy waters. At the same time he would try to comfort me: When you grow up, you can have your sailboat. But first, see that you finish high school.

To finish high school, now that was quite a tall order. I was weak in sciences, lousy in history, hopelessly bad at math, I was flunking practically every subject. With the exception, oddly enough, of Portuguese: I always did well in my compositions; the teacher, Maria Aparecida, whom we had nicknamed Turtledove, kept writing encouraging words on the margins of my notebooks. But in the same breath she would scold me: A shame that you're so lazy, Paulo. Lazy and inattentive.

No, there was nothing inattentive in the glances I kept casting at the teacher. Passionate, yes; she was—and she died without every knowing about it—my first love. I worshiped the Turtledove—a short, dark-complexioned young woman with large breasts and a sweet smile. It was for her that I excelled in my compositions, and if I succeeded, it was because of the subliminal messages of affection that I kept inserting between the lines. No, dear Turtledove, inattentive I was not.

Lazy, however, I was. I enjoyed sitting for hours on end at the edge of Pier C-3. While waiting for the fish to rise to the bait, I would gaze at the Greek freighters lying at anchor in the harbor and think of voyages to exotic places. Jerusalem, however, was not among them.

*   *   *

Jerusalem was on Benjamim's mind. I've known only one other person whose desire to travel surpassed mine, and this person was none other than Benjamim. He was one of those people who yearn to live in a city they've never seen, to marry a woman they've never met, to read a book that has never been written. You know the type, don't you? Benjamim yearned for Jerusalem. Why Jerusalem? you might well ask me, sir. Is it so different an experience to live in Jerusalem? So out of the ordinary? Sensible questions. Sensible, yes, except that they leave out history, quaintness.

To Benjamim, it was different; it made a world of difference. That's why we did for him what we did. That lunacy.

There I sat crying
as I remembered Sion
and all I had experienced there

—Camoëns

BENJAMIM'S FATHER OWNED A SMALL CLOTHING STORE ON
Rua Voluntários, almost across the street from our bar.

The family had come from Poland shortly before the war.
His father, Senhor Arão, was a slightly built, bald-headed
man with a protrusive nose and a frightened expression on his
face. He took it upon himself to stand at the door of his store
to attract passersby. "Here!" he would shout in a tone of voice
that was a mingle of enthusiasm and despair. "Here!"—the
hard struggle to make a living on Rua Voluntários, where there
were dozens of other stores like his, all of them carrying the
same striped and flowered shirts, the same socks, the same long
johns, the same denim pants. "Here!"—the cry of a shipwrecked
person, the stertor of a dying man, the howl of a wild beast
brought to bay; the *Dieu le veut* of the Crusaders, the *Shazam*
of Billy Batson, the ululation of the Cheyennes. The outcry of
the Maccabees and the trumpet of Joshua. "Here!" Where are
you, Cain? "Here! The elixir," echoed Peep-Less farther down
the street. "The herbal elixir, here, the genuine elixir." *Here*
and *elixir, elixir* and *here*—the street resonated with dissonant
cries, and in this battle Senhor Arão was at a disadvantage:
his voice was weak. He suffered from bronchitis, he had fits of
coughing. And a funny accent.

16

No, Senhor Arão couldn't rely exclusively on his voice.
During the lean end-of-the-month days, when he felt the
pinch, he would resort to aggressiveness and buttonhole a
passerby, holding on to his jacket: "Here! Come in here, I
have something you'll like!" Clinging like a leech to a potential
customer, Senhor Arão was sometimes dragged like this—a
crazed lover unwilling to let go—for a good ten meters before
he relinquished his prey.

If Senhor Arão was short and skinny, Dona Frima, his wife,
could only be big and fat; if he was busy fighting his battles
on the sidewalk, she could only be sitting behind the counter,
fanning herself with a Yiddish newspaper and complaining all
the time: about the heat, about the flies, about her back pain.
In the dining room—the living quarters were behind the
store—Benjamim would do his homework, scratching his
practically hairless skull with a pencil (his father, who feared
lice more than anything else, more even than pogroms, had the
barber shave off his son's hair). The boy would keep scratching
his skull, and at times he would even smack it, for that skull of
his bothered him a great deal: it creaked and squeaked like a
ship in a storm, overloaded as it was with dreams and visions.
Not that his imagination was any richer than mine; it wasn't.
His ghosts, however, were more visible: his Maccabees were
more real than the specter of Sisenando, the Mute. And his
king, Solomon, the one who had built the Temple with cedars
of Lebanon and gold from secret mines, this king Benjamim
revered far more than he revered Dutra, who was then the
president of Brazil.

As a teenager, Benjamim looked like his father: somewhat
taller and stronger, but with the same expression in his
eyes—half distrust, half fear. He had no friends, he didn't hang
out with any crowd. It wasn't until high school that he and I
became friends. We were in the same class at Júlio de Castilhos
High School. We always sat at the very back of the classroom,
but for different reasons: laziness in my case, shyness in his. As
a student he wasn't outstanding; besides, having been born in
Poland, he had a strong accent, and he rolled his r's heavily. He
stammered and blushed whenever he was asked to go to the
blackboard. And every once in a while he would come up with

something preposterous, like, *At sunset, the bull was dying*, a
sentence he composed when the teacher asked him to illustrate
the use of the imperfect tense. At sunset, the bull was dying.
Exactly.

In the history classes, however, he became transformed; as the
teacher discoursed on the Crusades, on the siege of Jerusalem,
he sat listening as if hypnotized, his mouth half open, his eyes
glittering. Overcoming his shyness, he would sometimes raise
his hand and ask the teacher permission to add to what she had
been saying. Far from being annoyed at the interruption, she
would invite him to come to the front of the classroom; then, as
he stood there, gesticulating a great deal and swaying his
body in that peculiar way of his, he would tell stories about the
Holy City, about Solomon, a just king, a poet-king, a monarch
with a thousand concubines. We weren't quite sure what
concubines were, but we guessed: a concubine ... Concubines!
One thousand! One thousand women in all colors and shapes—
but all of them sexy, of course—one thousand raving beauties
lying side by side on a bed (what a bed! how wide it must have
been!), all of them smiling, all of them reaching out their
arms, all of them saying something in Hebrew—but the meaning
was unmistakable—*Come here, sweetie*. One thousand women.
If one were to spend twenty, or fifteen minutes with each one
of them, how long would it take to ... ? A problem that our
math teacher never assigned us for homework.

Funny? Maybe. The fact is that nobody ever laughed at
Benjamim's stories, narrated in an intricate way; on the
contrary, we felt that we had before us a prophet, a visionary.
Nowadays I suspect that the Jerusalem he was always talking
about, that city of golden domes, of magnificent towers and
massive walls existed only in his head. We were, however,
impressed by that veneration of his, a veneration bordering on
fanaticism.

His fixation was probably due to the fact that before coming
to Brazil, his parents had considered immigrating to Palestine.
Like their son, Arão and Frima knew Jerusalem only from
photographs. Actually, not even from photographs, but rather
from etchings reproduced in an old book on Jewish history that

Arão owned; these etchings depicted the city in the eighteenth
century, but even so, it was seen in the distance, on the horizon.
In the foreground, near a palm tree, a man wearing a turban,
his back turned to the viewer, was facing the city. Although the
man's face was invisible, his figure translated at once the
melancholy and the serenity that the viewer could divine in his
gaze. It was at this etching that Arão and Frima would look
as they sat in the living room of their small house in Warsaw.
Holding each other tenderly, they would talk in whispers
about Jerusalem. At the sound of the whispered word, *Jerusalem*,
Benjamim would stir in his mother's womb; it was almost
certain that he was listening; it was almost certain that the
nostalgic gaze of the man wearing the turban was his, too.

Arão, a grandson and great-grandson of Talmudists, wished
he could live in Jerusalem, preferably near the Wailing Wall,
where he would pray daily—a mitzvah, a benediction, he
used to say, that would ensure him a place in heaven, in the
very bosom of Abraham. Frima, also the daughter of religious
parents, didn't entirely disapprove of the idea. Being more
down-to-earth, though, she often wondered where the money
to feed the family would come from; there was Nunho, already
a big boy, and now another child, Benjamim, was on the way.
Praying, that was fine and dandy; but what about feeding the
family? She gradually won her husband over to the idea of
trying their luck in America. First they would make a great
deal of money—then later, yes, Jerusalem. But Jerusalem with
security. Jerusalem with a good reserve fund that would enable
them to live the mystic adventure to the fullest. At first Arão
resisted this materialistic way of thinking. In Jerusalem, he
would say, God will provide for us, Jerusalem is the city of
miracles. Miracles, yes, Frima would reason, but ...

The war settled the matter for them. They had to flee, a
friend succeeded in getting them visas to enter Brazil. They
came to Porto Alegre. As time went by, they forgot Jerusalem,
the man wearing the turban, the book.

Benjamim didn't forget. Poor Benjamim.

A melancholy childhood.

Very early in life he had been severed from the maternal
bosom because Dona Frima didn't have enough milk to nurse
him. And this in spite of her huge breasts, which everybody
noticed and even joked about; mammoth breasts, under
which a whole crowd could find shelter from the rain; breasts
that made any feeding bottle with a nipple look plain
ridiculous, to say the least, no matter how delicious its contents.
Those breasts, so ample that they gave their owner a heat
rash in the summer, were unable to produce a single drop of
milk for poor Benjamim. In the absence of this terrific liquid,
the parents had to resort to various concoctions prepared in
accordance with ancient Jewish and Polish formulas; Benjamim
rejected them all, and as a result, he grew up frail. Throughout
his childhood he was assailed by a variety of germs. He was
taken ill with the measles, smallpox, whooping cough, the
croup, neuralgia—the latter probably as a result of a chilly
wind that blew from the river—not to mention typhoid, which
he contracted at the time of the floods of 1941. He survived
them all, only to be cruelly bullied by his brother, with whom
he shared the bedroom. There's no way this world can hold
both of us, the heartless Nunho would say as Benjamim, his ears
red, did his homework. Benjamim cut a sorry figure: his hair
cut short, his skin inflamed with pimples that kept sprouting all
over, his Adam's apple poking out of his throat, his neck
much too elongated. A pitiful sight, that is, until he started
talking about Jerusalem. Then the melancholy of that turbaned
Arab would leave him to be replaced by the exaltation of a
knight in search of the Holy Grail. By the magnificence of a
Solomon.

I got along well with Benjamim. In those days I used to
collect stamps, and he would bring me the envelopes of the
letters that his parents received from Europe, with beautiful
stamps inscribed with Cyrillic and other characters that I
didn't understand, but for this very reason the stamps were
even more precious to me. In exchange I would help him
with his compositions—he had tremendous difficulties with the

Portuguese language and he admired my flair for writing. He
intended to tell me all about his life so that I could turn it into
a novel. A short story; an article, at the very least.

With me he would open up. He would tell me about his
problems with his parents, who didn't understand him, and
his brother, who ill-treated him. This brother of his, this
Nunho, was well-known on Rua Voluntários: a tall, elegant
young man, always well dressed and perfumed, his hair, glossy
with brilliantine, carefully combed back—a dandy, a fop, a
coxcomb of a Jew, in short, a type in sharp contrast with
Benjamim. Peep-Less was always bad-mouthing Nunho, claiming
that he exploited women, that he was involved in smuggling.
His suspicions were quite pertinent: Nunho, who had moved
out of his parents' house to live in a posh apartment on Rua da
Praia, made a lot of money. Accompanied by mysterious
blondes bedecked with furs and jewels, he would cruise the city
center in a Mercury roadster full of chrome and antennas.
Money, that's all that matters to him, Benjamim, aggrieved,
would say.

Benjamim didn't want to have money, or even beautiful
women. His dream was to become a history teacher; but in
Jerusalem, he would add, rolling the *r*. He would make the
dream of his father, and of his father's father, come true: he
would live in an ancient house, near the Wailing Wall, and
he would spend his time praying, teaching, and researching old
documents.

It was an aspiration that I couldn't understand. To me
history was nothing but an endless, boring succession of dates,
of kings' names (which I could remember only if they had a
nickname tagged to them, such as the Great, the Fortunate,
the Beautiful, the Terrible), of battles, of treaties—none of
which interested me, except as possible examination questions.

To Benjamim, however, history was something else. He lived
it. History was part of the tradition of his people. Sighing, his
mother would recall the rabbis among her ancestors; his father
would wake up in the night, screaming—in his nightmares he

was being persecuted by Bogdan Chmielniky, an anti-Semitic
cossack who lived in the seventeenth century. Benjamim,
riding on a horse along with his King Solomon, would try in
vain to hurry to his father's assistance.

Benjamim's parents had other plans for him. They wanted
him to study engineering. At least one of their sons with a
university degree, they kept insisting, especially because Nunho—
sure, he was independent, and was making money by hook or
by crook, they'd rather not know the details—had dropped out
of school when he was still in elementary school.

As for Jerusalem, Benjamin wasn't even to contemplate the
possibility of living there. Under no circumstances would they
allow their son to leave Porto Alegre. Jerusalem? No way.
Certainly not while the Old City (it was 1951 then) was under
the control of Jordan. It was out of the question.

We used to talk about such matters on our way home from
school. We would walk all the way from Rua João Pessoa to
Rua Voluntários, via Rua Conceição. As we walked, I would
greet the merchants, friends of Father's, who stood at the
door of their wholesale businesses watching the black deliverymen,
their heads white with flour, their naked torsos glistening
with sweat, unload sacks of beans and rice from old trucks.

I remember clearly the first time Benjamim invited me to
his house. There's something interesting I'd like to show you,
he said, sounding mysterious.

We entered the store. He introduced me to his parents,
whom I already knew by sight. The couple exchanged
glances, a mixture of satisfaction (at long last Benjamim has
made a friend) and suspicion (was he a nice kid, this Paulo,
this son of the Portuguese bar owner, this goy?). Anyhow, they
treated me kindly, asked me to make myself at home.

We walked across the house. A small house, cluttered with
furniture, knickknacks, and old photographs: white-bearded
old men wearing hats and black cloaks; women with frightened
eyes, their heads covered with kerchiefs—Benjamim's ancestors.
At the back of the house was a small yard with a tiny storage

shed, inside of which was something he wanted to show me: a miniature replica of Jerusalem, which he had built himself with clay, pebbles, and slats; from the towers hung banners made of colorful paper. Full of emotion, he pointed out the Wailing Wall to me. One day I'll touch the stones of this Wall, he said with almost pathetic fervor.

IF I'M NOT MISTAKEN, I THOUGHT IT WAS ALL VERY INTERESTING, very beautiful; however, to the best of my recollection, at that moment I was thinking of something else—of women, as a matter of fact. In 1952, 1953? Women. That's all I could think of, women. And how could it have been otherwise? Not here, on Rua Voluntários da Pátria.

I used to help Father in the bar until seven or eight o'clock in the evening, when I had dinner. By then the blue-collar workers, the salesclerks, the government employees had already gone home. It was then that the women began to emerge from their bedrooms in the old two-story houses. They would walk slowly, balancing themselves on their high heels; or they would station themselves on the street corners, leaning against a wall. Or they would sit in dimly lit joints, their eyes sparkling in the near-darkness. This whole area was always teeming with women. A quick examination of the sensual geography of Porto Alegre would disclose a city occupied by this erotic army. On Rua Pantaleão Telles, near the stone bridge where the Farrapos, the insurrectionists of the 1835 Revolution, used to fight fiercely, there was a large contingent entrenched in the small houses of the Lower City. On Rua Azenha, the Cabo Rocha cabaret was an important stronghold. And in the

Cristal neighborhood, Mônica reigned solo and splendidly in her Mirror Room. But there were even more fantastic places, such as the "Cabaret of the Normal School Students," where, as rumor had it in Porto Alegre, the girls from the normal school would throw off their masks of innocence. Instead of the guileless gaze with just a touch of slyness, the suggestive wink of heavily painted eyes; instead of the navy-blue skirt and white blouse of the school uniform, a slinky, outrageous low-cut dress; instead of school songs, bawdy ditties. And everything for free, pleasure for pleasure's sake.

Ecstasies apart, the main contingent of women was to be found downtown, on Rua Voluntários. Women for all kinds of taste and in a wide range of prices to suit everybody's pocketbooks, except, alas, mine. Indefatigable, they kept pacing the turf far into the night. There they were: behind the Bank of Commerce with its imposing granite columns; behind the Post Office with its tower displaying a clock with a green dial; and even behind the Revenue Department Building—walking in silence, their shoulders hunched against the foggy winter night, stopping every once in a while to stomp their frozen feet on the sidewalk.

There was one who never walked. She would rather not walk. She always stood motionless, her eyes fixed on that big stone airplane perched on Rua Sete. That airplane was, as everybody knew, a gas station, but what she saw wasn't a gas station, what she saw was an airplane—made of stone or not—ready to take off. Closing her eyes, that girl would envision the airplane taking off, transporting her, as she stood in the aisle (for she imagined that airplanes were like buses), to a far-off country, where it would land in the middle of an immense, deserted prairie. She would alight, the airplane would take off again, and once in solitude, she would undress and lie naked on the soft grass, the heat of the sun gradually dislodging the chill from her bones. And then the young man would arrive, and she would open her arms to welcome this Paulo, who had come from far away, from Porto Alegre, as she had, too, in order to make love to her in that place, far from everything, and at a very affordable price: two or three *maravedis,* the currency of that distant country.

About women I knew everything there was to know. Syphilis, gonorrhea? By the age of ten I could have lectured on the subject. By the age of twelve, I was already sneaking into the Maipu and the Marabá cabarets, slipping in with the regulars. I would climb up the rickety stairs of the old houses, and there, immersed in an atmosphere clouded with cigarette smoke and reddened by the light of a few lamps, I would stand watching the compact mass of dancers undulating to the rhythm of the boleros played by a small, dissonant orchestra. The women, those women in slinky dresses, those heavily painted women, who languidly swayed their hips as they chewed gum, their eyes fixed, those women used to drive me crazy. Staggering down the stairs, I would run home, shut myself up in my bedroom, strip off, slip under the bed covers, and there I would lie, all atremble with excitement.

The night wind didn't bring me just the rasping sound of the streetcars running on steel rails (a sound that I can still hear to this day, before I drift off to sleep); it also brought me moanings of desire, giggles, murmurs. An appeal: *Come here, handsome boy, come here, Paulo darling, I've been waiting for you, sweetie, I have the hots for you.* Such a sweat appeal: somewhat phony, of course, somewhat melancholy, but to me, alone in bed at night, it was particularly alluring. Ah, did I ever lust for a woman! Any women would do, whether one of Solomon's concubines, or a hooker from Rua Voluntários, it didn't matter.

Women, lack of. No, the problem wasn't exclusively mine. It was everybody's problem, affecting the whole gang, the kids in my class, the friends from Caminho do Meio, from Rua Floresta, from downtown. A drama that reached its climax on Saturday nights.

On Saturday nights we wore, as was then fashionable, some really nifty clothes, outrageous neckties and loads of brilliantine. We would leave home and head for our usual hangout, the entrance to the Coliseu Movie Theater, where we would arrive at about seven o'clock, our eyes glittering, our faces

(almost always pimply) grinning broadly. We would greet
each other with the expressions then current—*Hey, where's the
dope?* or *What's the matter with your dickey?* We would call
each other names, it was the thing to do—you twerp, you leper,
you jerk, you twit, you drip.

Then we would enter the movie theater. We would sit
upstairs, in the peanut gallery. We would whistle and stomp
our feet; we were the terror of parents, who would threaten us
with the manager. Such threats would send us into peals of
laughter: If you don't like it, tough luck, we would say,
showing our contempt for conventions.

Although it was a double feature (with a break in between,
when the candy man came with his tray of coffee-and-milk
toffees) the movie session was soon over, and once again we had
to face our old problem, women. How could we get a
woman? In those days none of us knew; many still don't; others
have died without ever knowing. Some of us would suggest
picking up some lease pieces, a suggestion dismissed as
impractical—on foot, and with no moola, forget it! If an
older woman, in her thirties, no matter how ugly, gave one of
us the come-on, we would prod him on, half supportive, half
envious, it was the thing to do: Don't just stand there gaping,
go and get it, you have a hard-on for her, don't be such an
asshole! But generally speaking, the fellow would cower, muttering
the usual excuses: I know this old bag, she's married, her
husband is from the tough town of Bagé. Which would trigger
the usual gibes: our friend was all talk and no action, all he
did was fondle his fig and jerk off—an asshole, in short. The
insulted kid would then insist that he hadn't really missed out
on anything (an old cunt, that broad), and that sooner or later
he would get himself a dame. In those days nobody wanted to
be left without a woman.

We were randy for a hot patootie, dying to dance the buttock
jig—to use expressions then in vogue. But we were dead
broke. *Come here, sweetie,* the women would call out to us, but
we couldn't go to them. Dead broke, we were. We couldn't
even afford a bowl of chicken soup at the Treviso Coffee Shop,
or a roast pork sandwich at the Matheus, let alone pay for the

services of a streetwalker. By the end of the night we would
have been satisfied with anyone. Had a repulsive witch,
broomstick and all, suddenly materialized before us, we would
have kissed and embraced her as if she had been the most
charming normal school student, as if she had been the Queen
of Sheba herself. A midget, even a lame one, would have
served our needs. A ewe. A black sheep. A hen. A frog.

Nothing ever turned up, we never got anything, ours was a
hopeless case. We would return home and go to bed, a sour
taste in our mouths; and thus, on a melancholy note, ended our
nights in that period of our lives.

I couldn't bear being without a woman anymore. But what
about the money? Father didn't give me an allowance; he took
it upon himself to supply me with everything I needed—
clothes, books, notebooks. I was even thinking of stealing the
dough from the cash register; but then, just before my
fifteenth birthday, Father asked me what I would like as a gift:
a shirt, shoes? I'd rather have some money, sir, I said, amazed
at my own boldness. He looked at me steadily, without saying
anything. Then taking his wallet out of his pocket, he
counted some money and handed it to me.

That very night I went running to Elvira.

Long black hair, greenish eyes, full lips, pointed breasts—to
me she was the loveliest woman in the world, or at least as
beautiful as the actresses, whose pictures, cut out from the
Revista do Globo, I kept concealed in my notebooks (the only
thing in those notebooks that appealed to me). Yes, Lana
Turner was sexier, and Claudette Colbert sweeter, and Bette
Davis had that defiant gaze, and Rita Hayworth—ah, she was
something else, my passion, my perdition, I had seen Gilda three
times. But the movie stars were far away, and Elvira within
reach. True, she had fuzz on her upper lip, and a gold tooth,
and a deep voice with a foreign accent because she was from
one of the Italian settlements in the interior. But I saw her

every day, and more than once a day, and every time I
walked past her on Rua Voluntários she smiled at me: her
strong perfume (Coty something, I think it was) would haunt
me throughout the night. Elvira, I would moan, in bed. For a
long time I had been lusting for her. I had already spoken to
her several times, but I knew that with no money, nothing
doing. She was a regular at the Maipu Cabaret, and she was
in great demand; why would she pay any attention to the son
of the Portuguese bar owner?

That night, however, it was with self-confidence that I
climbed the stairs of the Maipu. And with anxiety, too; and if
she wasn't there? And if she was with someone else? Groundless
fears. She was there all right, and with no male companion:
seated at a table, she was chatting with other women. I drew
near.

"Good evening, Elvira." My voice sounded strange. "May I
have this dance, Elvira?"

She looked at me. "Got any dough, Paulo? No money,
nothing doing; I don't sell on credit, you know." With a
superior smile, I produced my wallet, crammed with bills.
Groaning softly, "Ouch, my hips, I feel rotten today," she rose
to her feet. "See you later, gals."

We danced away, cheek to cheek. Noticing that I was
aroused, she whispered in my ear, "Would you like to go to
my bedroom, sweetie?"

We went to her room, which was in a house a short distance
away. A big room, worthy of Elvira's self-importance. High
ceiling, lamps in the corners, numerous knickknacks, colorful
prints. On the bed, a big china doll, which Elvira kissed
before putting it aside. On a wall a crudely handwritten price
list. It began with *a quickie* and ended with *overnight stay*, the
prices rising accordingly. Would you like me to turn the lights
off? she asked. I said it wasn't necessary. We stripped and lay
down.

"Is it your first time?" She was smiling.

Oh, no, I said, pretending to be an old hand. I've been with
many others. I wanted to tell her some stories, but I got all
mixed up and ended admitting: Yes, Elvira, it's the first time.

Then leave it to me, she whispered. I did, and it was very good. Very good, indeed. She moaned as if she were coming, and maybe she really was, maybe at first she didn't want to come, but then she came in spite of herself; maybe it was her own moanings that aroused her, that made her come; maybe she preferred moaning to coming. I don't know and I'll never know. Anyhow, it was good.

As we got dressed, she started to tell me about herself. Because she wanted to; I didn't even try to make small talk. I had screwed her like a macho and I was happy, even proud, there was no reason why I should chat with the woman. But she wanted to talk, to tell me about her life, and so she did.

She hadn't been on Rua Voluntários very long. As a matter of fact, although she looked much older, she was only five years older than me. She had left her family, who lived in the interior, in the municipality of Bento Gonçalves, to come to Porto Alegre. Not that she disliked life on the farm, she said, her eyes fixed, the bra still in her hand. Yes, she had enjoyed working in the vineyards, picking grapes.

"But," she went on, "I became fed up with the whole thing. It was hard work, know what I mean? An awful lot of grapes to be picked. And not many distractions. Mass on Sundays, a church bazaar once in a while, a dancing party, no movies at all. I wanted some action, I wanted to be surrounded by people, know what I mean, Paulo? But out there, there were only my parents, my brothers, a quiet life, the daily grind."

She ended up running away from home. She came to Porto Alegre with a cousin of hers. The two girls found jobs as housemaids in the home of a lawyer, a certain Doutor Alfredo, who had two teenage sons—twins, they were. The lawyer went out almost every night; he belonged to a mysterious antisubversive organization, whose members held meetings sometimes at the home of this member, sometimes at the home of that member. As soon as the lawyer turned his back, his wife would also go out to meet her lover, an eccentric painter, a loner who lived on the same street. The twins would then challenge Elvira and her cousin to a pillow fight.

"And one of those fights was our undoing," she said.

Her cousin got pregnant, had to have an abortion, almost bled to death. When the lawyer heard about the case, he was furious and fired both girls. Her cousin was lucky; she later married a fireman. Elvira went from job to job. Like her cousin, she, too, would like to find a good man who would look after her. But he would have to be rich enough to give her dresses, a three-bedroom apartment, a car.

"Nonsense, Paulo. It's not my destiny to marry."

Elvira did, however, have a lover.

About this mysterious figure she hardly ever talked. By piecing together a word here, another word there (uttered with difficulty), some evasive answers, an occasional sigh, I began to visualize an eye, an outrageous mustache, a finger sporting a ring set with a red stone. A picture gradually emerged: a man, still young, probably about her age; a handsome but wicked man; a rat fink. A man who was indebted to her for everything he knew about sex, but who repaid her by beating her up (*once he beat me unconscious, and left me lying in a corner, all black and blue*). A man who had driven her, at least indirectly, into prostitution (*I told him I would sink into prostitution. He couldn't care less. I started turning tricks. Have been doing so ever since*). A man who had exploited her (*not that he ever asked me for money. He hardly ever talked to me, so he couldn't really ask me for anything, could he? But he accepted my gifts. And when I offered him dough, he took that, too. Without saying a word, without even thanking me*). A man to whom she had given everything, a man who left her for other women (*I know he's no good, but ...*), a man whom, in spite of everything, she still loved (*in spite of everything, I still love him*).

She wouldn't tell me the man's name. But random remarks led me to believe that at one time he must have lived on Rua Voluntários (*there was a time when I saw him every day, Paulo. And he would pretend he hadn't seen me, especially if he happened to be with his parents*), that he probably still frequented our street because there were days when she became distraught, acting like a madwoman.

"Ah, Paulo, I'm quite beside myself. Guess who I saw today."

It was Nunho. I never mentioned any of this to Benjamim, but there was no doubt in my mind, the man could only be Nunho. A ring set with a red stone? Him. An exploiter of women? Him.

Nunho, for sure. This explained why she would gaze so longingly at the inside of Senhor Arão's store, upsetting him and irritating Dona Frima. Who else but Nunho?

"And what about your family," I would ask, "do they know about you?"

Alarmed, she would look at me. "Heavens, no, Paulo! Heavens, no!"

Very religious people, they were. Of her six brothers, two were priests. The oldest, Francisco, lived in Palestine. Every year he would walk the Way of the Cross on his knees, kissing the stones on which Our Lord had walked.

"A saint. A real saint of a man. If my brothers knew I'm a hooker, I'm sure they'd kill me," she would say in a trembling voice.

Her family thought that she worked in a store. *I've sold lot a lot of taffeta this year*, she would write home, adding that she earned nice commissions on what she sold. Her parents would thank her for the money she sent them; things weren't too good on the farm, the price of grapes was down. "It's because of them that I must charge you, darling," she would say, counting the crumpled bills that I would hand her. Placing the money inside her bra, she would dismiss me with a kiss.

"Always come back, love."

I always went back. As soon as I had some money—which was no longer unusual, for my father had started giving me an allowance—I would run to the Maipu in the evening.

I never discussed such matters with Benjamim. With him the rap sessions were different: school matters, Jerusalem. Women? He rarely raised the subject. Ashamed, he would admit that he

didn't even go out at night. Merely asking his mother
permission to go to a movie was enough to throw her into a fit:
A movie? Absolutely not. I know you want to get mixed up
with women, you shameless creature! You want to kill your
mother, you killer!

Dona Frima would roll her eyes, raise her hands to her
breasts.

"Oh, me, Arão, I'm not feeling well. Arão, help me, I'm
dying, Arão! Arão, I'm dead!"

Benjamim and his father would help her to bed, fan her,
bring her water. In vain.

"Dead, Arão. I'm dead, Arão, good and dead. Feel the cold
of my hands, Arão. A dead woman's hands."

Raising her head, she would look at the glass of water, then
laugh theatrically.

"Water! They bring me water. What good will it do me,
Arão? Tell me, what good can water possibly do to a dead
woman? I'm dead, Arão. Good and dead. Your son has killed
me. This one here. This Benjamim. And do you think he
cares? Not at all. Women, that's all he cares about, this bandit.
He has killed his mother because of women."

"Calm down, Frima," Arão would beg of her. "You'll make
yourself sick with all this agitation, calm down."

"Calm down?" she would burst out. "So I'm not calm
enough, is that so, Arão? I'm more than calm, Arão, I'm
dead. Dead, Arão. Why don't you bury me once and for all,
Arão. He's in a big hurry to get to that cabaret."

Benjamim, his head lowered, would say nothing. He would
leave the room and return soon after, wearing his pajamas. At
this sight Dona Frima would suddenly feel better. Jumping out
of bed, she would grab her son, kiss him:

"Now, yes, my son! Now I know I won't die! You took pity
on your mother, Benjamim. Thank God."

Filled with sudden remorse for having yelled at him, she
would rush to the kitchen, and despite the late hour she
would start to prepare a meal: cheese pancakes, Benjamim's
favorite dish. Already in bed, he would stare at the ceiling,
and sigh.

*   *   *

One night, however, I ran into Benjamim on Rua Voluntários.
I was with Elvira; we were headed for her room.

Surprised, we looked at each other: in my case, because I had
never expected to see him out on the street at such a late
hour—midnight. Later I was to learn that his mother, as usual,
had made a scene that night—I'm dying, I'm dead—but
instead of rushing to her aid, Benjamim had grabbed his coat
and walked out of the house, much to the astonishment of his
parents. He decided that he had had it. He had no particular
destination in mind; he was just taking a walk, still frightened
at his action but already enjoying his freedom.

There he stood, looking at me, looking at Elvira. Obviously
hurt, because I hadn't told him I'd already been sleeping with
a woman. Without a word, he walked away.

At school on the following day, we kept glancing at each
other but we didn't talk. During recess, we sat side by side,
munching on our sandwiches, both of us ill at ease. Our mutual
embarrassment grew unbearable. Then all of a sudden the
two of us started talking at once, and it was about having run
into each other the night before; we laughed and laughed, we
were choking and coughing; and then we fell silent, only to
start talking again at once; and we broke into laughter.
Finally Benjamim spoke. He said that he was upset, that I
hadn't confided in him. And in the same breath, but choosing
his words carefully, he declared that he thought Elvira very
pretty.

I threw what was left of my sandwich on the ground. Shit,
Benjamim, stop pussyfooting, will you? If we can't level with
each other, who else is there? Shit, if you want to go with
Elvira, why the hell don't you just say so? Shit, you're my
friend!

Yes, he wanted to go with Elvira. Okay, I said, repressing my
jealousy. I'll take you to Elvira. We looked at each other, we
laughed, he punched me on the chest, I punched him back, he
tottered, I was much stronger. Friends again.

And is it good? he wanted to know. Good what? I asked.
Well, you know, this business with women. There was a tone
of concern in his voice, of anxiety mingled with excitement: a

navigator about to set sail for unknown lands. Of course, it is, I said, it's always good, women. He: Very good? Very good, I assured him.

It was all settled then, but there was a snag: Benjamim's father wouldn't give him the money. To spend on women? No way. My old man doesn't approve of such things, Benjamim said, he's afraid I'll catch some disease, that I'll fall in love with a goy, or heaven knows what. And what about your brother? I asked. Benjamim closed his face: He's a fucking bastard, I wouldn't want anything from him.

I hadn't been able to get anything from my father. Not until next week, he had said, right now I'm pinched for money. Seated on the edge of the wharf, Benjamim and I were staring dejectedly at the rotten oranges that were floating on the dirty water. And then it occurred to me: There's no other way, you'll have to filch the dough. Alarmed, he looked at me; the idea of stealing had never crossed his mind. Steal from whom? From your store, I said, from where else? A bank? But he kept stubbornly shaking his head; he wouldn't steal. He couldn't. No way. I lost my temper: Then remain a virgin for the rest of your life, I yelled. Rising to my feet, I walked away.

At school on the following day he beckoned to me. We went to the washroom, where he showed me a ten-cruzeiro bill. I've already started, he said, ashamed, but with a certain pride. It took him a long time to raise enough money. There were times when he would chicken out; sometimes, with his hand already in the till (his parents at home, eating lunch), he would waver, and end up beating a retreat. I spoke to Elvira. How much has he got? she asked, half amused, half suspicious. I told her. After mulling it over, she said: Okay, bring him over, we'll solve his problem for good. This kid looks like a lunatic; he must be choking his gopher something fierce, and that's not good.

We went to the Maipu. From a table, Elvira waved at us, smiling. Go, I said to Benjamim. Startled, he looked at me: Will it work out all right, Paulo? Sure it will, I reassured him, go now, she's waiting.

He went. They danced for a while—Benjamim quite clumsy—
then they left together.

I sat drinking. I drank a great deal: several cognacs with beer
chasers. Half an hour later Benjamim was back, looking pale,
bug-eyed. How did it go? I asked, already half drunk. The
woman refused to go with me, he mumbled. What? It didn't
make sense; I thought he was pulling my leg or something. It's
true, he said, she took the money, said she wouldn't do it, she
didn't feel like screwing. When I complained, she pulled a
razor on me.

Leaping to my feet, I grabbed a bottle by the neck and hit it
against the table, like in the movies. Unfortunately the bottle
slipped out of my hand and hit a woman who was dancing.
Watch out, you animal, she yelled, are you trying to kill me
or what? Grabbing another bottle, I did the same thing again
and this time I succeeded. I was holding the jagged bottleneck
in my hand. A deadly weapon. Let's go, I shouted.

The orchestra stopped playing; all eyes were turned to us. I
walked across the dance hall, followed by Benjamim who was
begging me to simmer down. We left and went to Elvira's
room. I kicked the door open. She was sitting before the
mirror, preening herself. What did you do to my friend here,
you whore?

Astounded, she looked at me. "Who, me? Are you kidding?
Me? I did nothing. He couldn't get it up and he walked
away."

"He couldn't?"

I turned around. Benjamim had vanished from sight. Puzzled,
I sat down on her bed. So poor Benjamin couldn't get it up.
You must have been mean to him, I insisted. I was not, said
Elvira. He's got himself to blame if he couldn't get it up, he
had a bad case of the jitters. And what about the money? I
asked. She laughed: Ah, darling, there's no refund, you know
that you don't toy with such matters. Now, he can come back if
he wants to. Then tell him so, I demanded.

We walked down the stairs. Benjamim was standing at the
front door. When he saw us, he wanted to bolt, but I held
him back: Wait, kiddo, be a man, will you? Elvira was

laughing, Benjamim was sulking, but ended up laughing, too.
Then holding him by the hand, Elvira led him upstairs.

I stood waiting. Minutes later they reappeared; he was
beaming: Now, yes, Paulo, now everything's fine.

We went back to the Maipu. Sitting at our table was a man
drinking beer. He was wearing a blue woolen pea jacket,
with golden buttons on it, and a captain's hat. It was the
Captain.

I'VE SAILED THE SEVEN SEAS, THE CAPTAIN TOLD US LATER
that night. And: What you kids know from books, I know
from having been there. I know Hong Kong, my dears. I
know Hong Kong inside out, every single street, every single
alley. I know Tokyo, I know Bombay.

Bombay held no secrets for him. Hamburg? No secrets
either. About Istanbul he knew everything there was to
know.

That he must have lived life to the hilt was clear from the
tortured expression on his face, a face that bore deep lines,
and perhaps even scars. His reddish nose and trembling hands
indicated that what he had to drown in booze was considerable.
Women ... the death of a buddy in the course of a nocturnal
battle fought against pirates in the Persian Gulf ... treachery!

A strong friendship was to develop from that first encounter.

Initially, however, I was in no mood to strike up a friendship
with him. In fact, I was trying to pick a fight. I searched for
a pretext: This table is ours, I said, in a challenging tone.

The Captain fixed his blue, bloodshot eyes upon me. He was
a middle-aged man, but still hale and hearty. He could have
demolished me right then and there, as he had done to the
Gorilla Man in Cape Town. Had he wanted to, he could have

sent me flying through the window of the dance hall, as he had
done to three cops in Macao. But he had no intention of
hitting a cocky kid. To the best of my knowledge, he said in a
cool, drawling voice, the tables here at the Maipu are not
anybody's property. Besides—and he smiled—you people are
welcome to sit at this table, there's plenty of room for
everybody. That's right, said Elvira, let's sit down, there's no
reason to fight.

Benjamim sat down; rather disconcerted, I sat down, too. The
Captain called the waiter, ordered more beer.

He had won us over. Benjamim, who had all of a sudden
become garrulous, kept bombarding the Captain with questions
about his voyages, about the places he had visited. Upon hearing
that the Captain had been to ancient Palestine, Benjamim was
all fired up.

"I was there," said the Captain, "let me see, in February . . .
no, it was March, 1948. I went there as the first mate on the
Kypros, the oldest and the most ramshackle freighter ever to sail
across the Mediterranean. A hazardous voyage it was. A cargo
that had to be delivered, no matter what. But I was handsomely
paid, see what I mean? Handsomely paid, indeed."

Enthralled, Benjamim sat staring at him.

"What kind of cargo was it?" I asked.

"Weapons, kid. Czech weapons: rifles, machine guns. Dangerous
little toys. Several tons of explosives. Two airplanes, dismantled.
Everything carefully packed in innocent-looking containers.
Powdered Milk, that's what was written on them, in English
and French. Powdered milk, kid. Can you imagine? We set sail
from Genoa. Nobody on board, with the exception of the
captain and myself, had any idea about what we were transporting.
When the sailors found out about it, they were terrified, and
planned an uprising. Ever seen a mutiny on board a ship?
Really ugly, my dear fellow. Very, very ugly. Picture this
scene: a stormy night off the coast of Cyprus, the ship heaving
like you wouldn't believe it. The men assembled on the deck:
Greeks, Portuguese, Italians, Spaniards, Turks, Chinese. Callous
types, many having several deaths on their shoulders.
Vociferating, hurling threats at us. They wanted to come to

anchor at La Valeta and unload the weapons there—or else they would cast us into the sea. A really ugly scene, kid."

The Captain filled his glass with beer, then took a swig.

"On the bridge, the skipper. Andreas. A Jewish Greek. A former guerrilla. A courageous man, hard, cold. The men raging and he just watching, without a word. His black beard sprinkled with raindrops. His eyebrows, too. He had bushy eyebrows, and his eyes—like coal, like real live coal. To Malta, the men were shouting. He, silent. Slowly they drew closer, some with large knives in their hands, others wielding clubs."

"And he? And the captain?" Benjamim couldn't contain his anxiety.

"He," said the Captain, "he just stood silent, with his arms folded. When the men were fairly close, one of them was already climbing up the stairs leading to the bridge, the captain opened his pea jacket—a pea jacket like this one here—and pulled out a machine gun. I'll fire at the first one who moves another step, he shouted."

The orchestra was playing a tango. Glued to each other, couples were sliding along the dance floor. Seated next to Elvira, I was engaged in some heavy petting, kissing her on the throat, on the neck, nibbling at her earlobes. Ah, Elvira, I kept whispering, what a hard-on I have for you. Benjamim wasn't paying attention to me (or was he just pretending?), his eyes riveted on the Captain, who had resumed his narrative.

"Up to that moment I had been undecided. I admit I had been undecided. But seeing the braveness, the courage of that man, I couldn't hesitate anymore. See, it wasn't a question of friendship. I wasn't a friend of his, at least not until that very moment. He was, after all, a Jew, and I, being of German descent and having several Nazi relatives, had always felt an aversion to Jews, see what I mean? However, what was at stake there was not the person, but the principle. So I drew my revolver and stood by him. You wretches, I shouted, if you kill the captain, you'll have to kill me, too."

"Gee," Benjamim kept mumbling, flabbergasted. "Gee." The Captain lit his pipe.

"Good, this pipe here. From the roots of a rosebush. English-made. A-1. I won it from a Malay. In a bet . . . Anyway,

that's irrelevant. So where was I? Ah, yes: You'll have to kill
me, too, that's what I shouted. I remember the scene as
clearly as if it had happened today. You'll have to kill me, too.
Yep, exactly. You'll have to kill me, too."

"Weren't you afraid, sir?" Benjamim asked.

"Afraid, kid?" The Captain broke into laughter. "I was
scared shitless. Know what it's like? Well, I was scared
shitless. I'm not ashamed to say, I was scared shitless. I was
shaking so badly I could hardly hold the revolver in my hand.
Fortunately my voice remained steady: You'll have to kill me!
The men stopped in their tracks. They exchanged glances,
they confabbed with each other. Our captain, motionless. Like a
statue. The men retreated, and returned to their posts."

"But," I cut in, "did you guys deliver those weapons or not?"

The Captain looked at me, annoyed at the untimely
interruption.

"Take it easy, lad! Do you think that delivering weapons is a
simple matter? That it's like delivering a box of bonbons?
No, kid. Weapons are dangerous. There were lots of people
keeping an eye on that cargo: Jews. Egyptians. Smugglers. A
shipful of them had been following us ever since we sailed from
Genoa. As a matter of fact, there was even a Russian
submarine. Not to mention the mysterious airplane that kept
wheeling over us ... But the worst of it were the English."

"The English were friends," muttered Peep-Less, who was
sitting at the next table, eavesdropping.

The Captain turned to him, "Ah, yes? Friends, you say? And
whose friends, mister? Can you tell us?"

"My former boss," mumbled Peep-Less, "had several English
friends. Folks from the meat-packing plant. Nice people.
Friends, they were."

"Friends!" The Captain thumped his fist on the table. The
bottle of beer fell over, the orchestra stopped playing, everybody
turned to stare. "Friends! Listen, the English have been never
anybody's friends! Never!"

"On with the music!" somebody shouted, and the orchestra
broke into "El Manisero."

"The English," went on the Captain, now calmer, "were after
our weapons. We knew they were. But before we set sail,

Andreas said to me: I'll deliver these weapons, even at the cost of my own life."

The Captain drained his glass dry, and made a grimace.

"It could have been colder, this beer here. Andreas. A swell guy. The best captain I've ever known. I first met him here in Porto Alegre; for a while, he had worked for my father, who owned a shipping company. During the great flood of 1941 Andreas bet with a friend that he would take a tugboat right to the city center. No sooner said than done. Steering the boat all by himself, Andreas slowly sailed past the Majestic Arcades, turned into Rua Sete de Setembro, and reached the Galeria Chaves Arcades—the only thing he didn't do was to make the tugboat climb up the stairway, everything else he did. A great captain. We'll sail right under the nose of the Englishmen, he had said to me, and so he did. About ten kilometers off the coast of Palestine we were enveloped by a dense fog. You couldn't see a thing. Very well; anyone else would have receded. Andreas, however, moved forward. We sailed past the English cruisers and arrived safe and sound at the appointed place, there to deliver the weapons."

"Did you deliver everything?" Benjamim was now ecstatic.

"You bet, kid. The weapons, the ammunition, the airplanes, everything. And we received a substantial amount of money. But Andreas didn't keep a single cent for himself. We took the money to some relatives of his who lived in Jerusalem."

"In Jerusalem?" Benjamim jumped out of his chair. "Have you then been to Jerusalem, sir?"

"Of course I have," said the Captain, taken aback. "What's the problem? I've been to Jerusalem. And why not? Jerusalem. Sure, I've been there."

Benjamim was begging the Captain to tell him about Jerusalem. This friend of yours is nuts, Elvira whispered in my ear, and I: Love. What a dish you are, love.

"Jerusalem," said the Captain. "Jerusalem. What can I tell you about Jerusalem? An interesting city. Very interesting. Historical. I myself don't care for historical cities, give me an exotic city anytime, Hong Kong, Tokyo, Bombay. But I'll acknowledge that Jerusalem has its merits. Ah, that's for sure. History galore there. A lot of monuments, a lot that is . . .

well, enigmatic. A city imbued with mystery. It's something we
sense, this mystery, it's something hard to explain. But what
really counts there is history. Many an ancient building. Age-old
stones, a thousand years old. If not more. If not more, eh? In
addition, there's this thing about Christ. Ah, sure: Christ. The
life of Christ, his passion, his death. I'm not religious, kid, I
stopped believing in this cock-and-bull story a long time ago,
but I've seen many a Christian crying in Jerusalem, and take
it from me, kid, it really gets to you. Christians crying. It really
gets to you. Crying like children. People there are very
devout. Very much so. A serious matter, yes, sirree."

"And the Wall?" asked Benjamim.

"What wall?" The Captain was puzzled.

"*The* Wall! The Wailing Wall! The most important thing,
the most ..."

"Oh, yes. The Wailing Wall. Sure, the Wall. Quite something,
that Wall ... An impressive thing, those stones ... And very
well built. It has withstood the passage of time ... of centuries.
Historical, that Wall."

This Captain is a liar, Elvira whispered in my ear. The only
boat he's ever been on is this tugboat of his, and even so, he
has rented it out.

"Tell me some more about the Wall," Benjamim urged the
Captain. "Did you get to touch it, sir?"

"Of course I touched the Wall, lad," said the Captain, rather
irritated by all that questioning. "Why wouldn't I touch the
Wall? I touched the Wall for a long time. With both my
hands."

"And?" asked Benjamim, eager.

"And what?"

"And the sensation?"

"The sensation? Well, quite a sensation, it goes without
saying. The Wall has an emotional impact on you. Even I,
who am a cold fellow, was affected by the Wall. You can
imagine what it did to Andreas. He was in tears. Andreas
cried. I didn't, of course. I was touched, but I didn't cry. But
Andreas cried. No wonder. The Wall ... Something
unbelievable. I've heard that touching the Wall brings luck."

"It does?" Benjamim found it odd. "Touching the Wall brings luck?"

"To some," the Captain amended. "Not to everyone. To some."

"Funny," said Benjamim, "I'd never heard it said that the Wall brings luck."

"The English bring luck," muttered Peep-Less, his head lowered to his chest, and the Captain growled: "Shut up, you sot, or would you rather have me bang that bazoo of yours shut?"

"Gee whiz," Benjamim kept murmuring. "Jerusalem. Wow."

"Ah, that's for sure," agreed the Captain. "Jerusalem is quite something. Only people who've been there can say it: Jerusalem is really quite something."

The Captain recalled a detail.

"So much so that Andreas decided to settle down there. No kidding, my lad! He settled down there; he didn't want to go back to his homeland. He accompanied me to the harbor and asked me to take the ship back to Genoa, where I was to sell it—and divide the proceeds among the crew. That's what Captain Andreas was like: kind, generous. It was a painful leavetaking, kid. The rest of us went on board, leaving him in the city he was so fond of."

"Wait a moment," protested Benjamim. "There's no harbor in Jerusalem."

"What?" said the Captain.

"There's no harbor there. Jerusalem is a long way from the sea."

"Ah, so it is." The Captain poured himself some more beer. "And did I say that it was near the sea? Come on: did I say it was?"

"No, but . . ."

"Did I say there was a harbor in Jerusalem?" The Captain was flying off the handle again. "What I said was that Captain Andreas accompanied me to the harbor. Those were my very words. Did I say there was a harbor in Jerusalem?"

Benjamim was at a loss for words. The Captain was now launching into a harangue.

"Do you think then that I don't know there's no harbor in

Jerusalem? Go fly a kite, kid! Would I not know then, a man
like me, that there's no harbor in Jerusalem? A man who has
sailed the Seven Seas? Stop bugging me, kid. What you
people know from books I know from having seen with my
own eyes, is that clear?"

Then, more subdued:

"True, I haven't been sailing lately. I'm a marked man, the
big companies hate my guts, they've boycotted me—I don't
know to what extent the English are behind this machination,
they're such vindictive types. At the very most, I'm allowed to
command my tugboat. Well, at least it's something. Something
to remind me of the days I used to spend on the high seas."

He drained off his glass.

"You know what? On these foggy winter nights, I occasionally
board a streetcar, and take the front seat next to the conductor.
As the two of us advance through the fog, it seems to me that
I'm again on board the *Kypros*, at Andreas's side, that we're
sailing for Palestine, that we're slipping right under the noses of
the Englishmen. Neat, isn't it, kid?"

"It sure is," granted Benjamim as he wiped his eyes, moved.
All of a sudden he was startled. "What's the time?" he asked.

"The time?" The Captain, who had been ruminating on his
memories, abruptly regained his composure. "What's the
time?"

He pulled out of his vest pocket an enormous, magnificent
watch, which immediately caught our attention. It was all
hammered silver, with a case cover on which was engraved the
coat of arms of the ancient and highly regarded Hanseatic
League, as I later learned. When the cover clicked open, it
produced a tune, a sweet, melancholy melody, which was
almost drowned out by the strident orchestra then playing a
mambo. The dial of this watch had Roman numerals, fancifully
designed hands, and the name of the manufacturer in Gothic
letters.

"It stopped," said the Captain, disappointed. He raised the
watch to his ear, shook it: nothing. Then he wound it with a
tiny key, listened again, and his face lit up.

"It's working again," he said. "Three hundred years old and
in perfect working condition. German-made. An heirloom

from my great-grandfather." The Captain sighed. "They don't
make watches as they used to in the old days."

But what time is it? Benjamim, increasingly restless, kept
asking. "Cut it out, will you, Benjamim?" said Elvira. "What
does it matter what time it is? You'll be late anyway. Relax,
enjoy yourself. Tonight is a special occasion. It's not every day
that people have their cherry popped, you know."

On that night, strange, disturbing impressions were still in
store for me. Half-drunk, with my head on Elvira's shoulder, I
suddenly fixed my gaze on Benjamim's left eye. An eye that
was to impress me deeply. Even more than his mouth, hanging
half open; even more than his protruding Adam's apple,
which kept rising and falling as Benjamim swallowed.

What I saw was a dilated pupil; the pupil of a blind man.
That left eye (maybe the right one, too, I couldn't tell) was
riveted on the Captain, but it didn't see him. Someone endowed
with a magician's eye (perhaps the man wearing the turban),
upon peering through that pupil the way others peer through
scuttles, would perhaps see the city of Jerusalem inside that
eyeball. Like one of those miniatures enclosed in a glass globe;
like one of those ship models built inside bottles (sailing ships
like the *Cutty Sark*, liners like the *Titanic*, aircraft carriers like
the *Saratoga*; galiots, caravels, barges). Yes, the city of Jerusalem:
domes, walls, temples, towers, arches, alleys, pilgrims, merchants—
everything. Rabbis, muezzins. Everything inside that eye.
Even Solomon's palace.

Reveries—nothing wrong with them. Jerusalem visualized—
fine; walls, towers—great. What surprised me unpleasantly
was the fascination that the Captain had kindled in Benjamim.
All right, I was jealous. Jealous but concerned, too, for there
was something wild in Benjamim's gaze.

Then, activated perhaps by my resentful gaze, the pupil in
Benjamin's eye began to contract, and his gaze, returning to
the reality of the Maipu, met mine. It was his turn to feel
jealous when he saw me amorously embracing Elvira.

*   *   *

His gaze was to become vacant again—a manifestation of
his preference for the previous state of remoteness, of sublime
indifference. Again he would be yearning for that mythical,
miniature Jerusalem inside him. Across unknown seas he would
be sailing for Jerusalem, his imaginary boat propelled by the
Captain's narrative. At such moments, in a fit of anger, I would
entertain the idea of assailing this fool's ship with my valiant
brigantine.

(A brigantine? Did I at one time in my life entertain the
idea of building a brigantine, even an imaginary one? Perhaps.
But I never even went as far as beginning to build one.
Neither did I ever cut down, in my imagination, the oak
trees—imaginary—for the imaginary hull.)

Yes, for one moment on that night I felt strange. As if the
music had suddenly stopped, as if the dancing couples had
suddenly frozen still under an unreal light. For one moment I
felt as if I were suspended between the sky and the earth—
Benjamim and I, the two of us divested of our bodies, of our
arms, of our legs, the two of us transformed into two big eyes:
planets in space.

For one moment. Soon, vibrant chords broke the spell.

"They're playing the carnival hit, the 'Jardineira'!"
Elvira jumped to her feet: "It's carnival time, folks! Carnival
time!" She shuffled toward the dance floor, and the five of
us—Elvira, myself, Benjamim, the Captain, and Peep-Less—
became a group of carnival revelers. Others joined in and
soon everybody was cavorting so merrily that it wasn't until
years later, at Turquinho's Cabana Nightclub, that we would
experience anything similar. It was three o'clock when we left
the Maipu, singing, with our arms around one another.
Afterward, the two us, Benjamim and I, sat on the curb, staring
at the paving stones of the street.

*   *   *

Beautiful, those stones, those granite paving stones in a
variety of hues, ranging from dark gray to pink, damp from the
fog, glistening in the weak light of the lampposts.

Today those stones are gone. They've been covered with
asphalt. It's progress; cars run smoother now. There are
people who don't like asphalt; I do. Asphalt has a beauty of its
own. An asphalt road at dawn, with its uniform, rippled
surface so clean—the wind sweeps it—stretching away out of
sight. Beautiful, yes.

I feel sorry for the stones. Personally, however, I find it
reassuring to know that they are there, intact, silent, hidden
under the asphalt. They're waiting for the day of the final
convulsion, the day when the earth will split open and all the
lost granite paving stones will reappear, embedded in the spaces
between the vertebrae of the fossilized prehistoric animals
that used to run along this very Rua Voluntários, long before
there ever was a streetcar named *Navegantes*—Navigators—
which would pass at dawn, carrying a few passengers: an old
man asleep, a public servant reading the newspaper, the ticket
collector chatting with the conductor. The streetcar that I see
nowadays, the one that traverses the light dreams of the
predawn hours, is not like the *Navegantes* streetcar; it's a vehicle
like the *Navegantes* streetcar, and like it, it has a big *N* on
the destination sign, but it's not as noisy, it doesn't pass with a
clatter of iron fittings, it doesn't sway on the steel rails.
Silently it emerges from the fog and silently it disappears into
it, the ticket collector and the conductor, side by side, looking
rather like the captain and the first mate of a ghost ship.

When I arrived home, I found Father waiting for me. This
time you've gone too far, he said. Oh shucks, get off my back, I
replied, and made for my room.

Grabbing me by the arm, he hit me. He struck me with his
Mozambican whip. It was just a token whipping; it didn't
hurt. But I ran to my bedroom, crying. I cried until it grew
light. I didn't go to school, I didn't get out of bed. My
mother, worried, came in with food. Go away, I said, I'm
through with all of you.

In the evening, after returning from work, Father went to
my room. He sat down on the edge of the bed and hugged
me. We apologized to each other, but something had been
shattered; things were no longer the same between us. As I
lay in bed grieving, the thought of running away from home
must have crossed my mind at one moment, and having
entertained this idea, I could no longer be the same person. A
ship leaving the harbor, disappearing on the horizon: I
thought a great deal about this.

Days later, in class, I noticed that Benjamim was restless;
he kept fidgeting on his seat, grimacing. He asked permission to
leave the classroom. He left, and was soon back—looking
frightened. What's wrong? I asked, and he, in a low voice: I'm
afraid I've caught some disease from that woman. Can't be, I
said, Elvira is very clean, I'm sure.

Excusing ourselves, we left the classroom together, under the
suspicious eyes of the teacher and amid the laughter of our
classmates. We went to the washroom. Benjamim showed it to
me: indeed, he had a discharge. Pee there for a while, I said,
knowing the score. He tried, groaning with pain. I asked if he
had been peeing against the wind, or walking barefoot on
cement. No, he hadn't done any such things.

There was no doubt about it, Benjamim had gonorrhea, all
right, and he could only have caught it from Elvira. Luckily I
had been spared, but even so I was furious. Why didn't that
cow take care of herself? Why didn't she see a doctor?

"So?" asked Benjamim, distressed. "What am I going to do?"

Leave it to me, I said. After school I took him to a drugstore
near Rua Voluntários. The owner, a diminutive bald-headed
man with eyeglasses, looked at us ironically: the problem was
plain as the nose on Benjamim's face. I waited until a lady
who was weighing herself moved away, then leaning on the
counter, I said in a confidential tone: My friend here has
caught a disease, could you help him? Benjamim, his ears red,
kept his eyes on the floor. The pharmacist searched through
the shelf for some medicine: There you are, a surefire cure, he
assured us.

It was a terribly expensive antibiotic. All the money we had
on us wasn't enough to pay for even one single capsule of the
medicine. Couldn't you, sir . . . ? I ventured. No, the man said
decidedly. He returned the bottle to the shelf.

"Come back when you have the cash."

The old prick! But he has already paid for it, poor fellow.
He died. Of an infection that was resistant to all kinds of
antibiotics, the ones he had in his drugstore and many others as
well. Poor fellow. He has already paid for it.

We left the store and walked aimlessly until we found
ourselves in Redenção Park. From their cages the animals—
flamingos, monkeys, catamounts—watched us. Benjamim, dejected,
walked with his head bowed. I tried to cheer him up: It's
going to be all right, buddy, we'll find a way.

We sat down on a bench and began to think of ways of
raising money. Several ideas occurred to me. We could
borrow money from the Captain, or even ask Elvira to pay us
an indemnity; after all, she was the culprit. It's no good, said
Benjamim with a sigh. I'll have to tell my father; I'll ask him
for the dough, and God's will be done. . . .

On the following day he showed up at school with a black
eye. He told the teacher that he had walked into a wardrobe;
at recess he told me he had gotten a beating. Not from his
parents; from his brother. The bastard thrashed me soundly,
Benjamim said, his voice trembling. He looked at me, full of
indignation.

"He, of all people, Paulo! He, who's always mixed up with
women. Tell me, Paulo, do you think it's fair? Is it fair,
Paulo? Is there no justice in the world, Paulo?"

"Gosh," I said. "But did he cough up the money?" I asked.

Yes, his brother had given him the money. I accompanied
Benjamim to the drugstore, we bought the medicine, I made him
take the first dose right there. A few days later he was well again.

I stopped going to the Maipu for a while. I was fond of
Elvira, I missed her, I even dreamed about embracing her; but
the fear of catching the disease won out, it was a sexual
turnoff.

One afternoon, as I was leaving the bar, I saw her on the street walking toward me. I escaped into a store, but she came after me and wanted to know what was wrong: You guys are sure making yourselves pretty scarce these days. I stammered an excuse—exams at school—but then all of a sudden, in a fit of rage, I got everything off my chest; I told her about Benjamim's disease, about our distress over the difficulty we had had in getting him the medicine.

"I don't want a dose of the clap, Elvira. I'm sorry; I like you a lot but there's no way I'm going to ruin my health."

Much to my surprise she burst into tears, right there in the store, under the astonished eyes of the salesgirls and the shoppers. Still crying, she went out into the street, and I followed her out, not knowing what to do. We went to her room, where she flung herself upon the bed, sobbing.

"It's a shitty life, Paulo. A real shitty life."

Mumbling vague excuses, I kept stroking her cheeks, her hair. And then I became horny and tried to unbutton her blouse. She pushed me away, not violently, but firmly: No, Paulo. Better not.

"I'll seek medical treatment. First-class treatment, with a specialist. And I'll be doing a lot of praying, too, and penance at the Shrine of Our Lady of Gloria. What's been happening to me is punishment, Paulo, punishment for the kind of life I lead. How could I, when I have two brothers who are priests? I'm nothing but a low-class hooker, Paulo."

Poor Elvira. The disease was one more letdown to be added to the long list of disappointments and unfulfilled dreams already grieving her. She would have liked, for instance, to have a bigshot as a lover—a banker, a doctor, a member of the Chamber of Deputies. But no, she had to content herself with the petite bourgeoisie: shopkeepers who were sometimes insolvent debtors; sales representatives, public servants. The most outstanding among her clients was Doutor Alfredo, who, years after having fired her, sought her out on the recommendation, as he told her, of a friend. After ascertaining himself that neither she nor any of her clients were communists, he started visiting her once a week. He would come wearing a disguise (*one must be careful not to give the Reds ammunition for*

their rhetoric): dark glasses, a false mustache, a hat with a
floppy brim, an overcoat with the collar turned up. Entering the
room together with Elvira, he would then search it thoroughly.
He would open the wardrobes, peer behind the curtains, look
under the bed. These people are no laughing matter, he
would say by way of explanation. The inspection over, he would
throw himself upon Elvira without even undressing; a
premature ejaculation, and presto, he would be on his feet
again, peeping at the street through the window. You wouldn't
believe some of these johns, Elvira would comment afterward.

She disliked Rua Voluntários: it had no class. She would
rather work at a place like Mônica's, in the district of Cristal.
Mônica, now that was a magical name, aristocratic even in the
way it was pronounced. Elvira had never met Mônica. She
imagined her as a tall, elegant lady, her blond hair carefully
done, with diamond-studded hoop earrings hanging from her
earlobes, a genuine pearl necklace with an antique cameo
adorning her lightly powdered bosom, an aura of French
perfume enveloping her figure.

And what about Mônica's Place? Elvira visualized what it
must be like: a mansion in the middle of a park. High walls,
a wrought-iron gate, armed guards. A driveway. A marquee. A
doorman in livery opening the door. A lobby done in Roman
marble. A receptionist stepping forward, eager to receive the
hats, the fur-trimmed overcoats, the silver-headed walking
sticks (and rapiers?), the white silk scarves. Distinguished
habitués: senators of the republic, well-known professionals,
financiers, representatives from the productive classes: captains
of industry, big wheels of the business world, prosperous
ranchers. Courteous, educated men. In a soft voice, they would
chat with Mônica's girls (refined girls, many of them former
normal school students, who wore silk and satin), as the girls
languidly reclined on chaises longues, puffing at their cigarettes
with amber holders.

And the bedrooms. Ah, the bedrooms! Elvira had heard
wonders about those bedrooms, magnificently decorated (fur
rugs, crystal chandeliers, hardwood furniture, fireplaces, bathrooms
done in marble), each room in a different style. There was
one in particular that roused her curiosity—and envy. The

Mirror Room, *all* of it—ceiling, walls, floor—covered with crystal mirrors. At any given moment and from every possible angle, a couple could watch themselves making love. In the Mirror Room the lovers were, so to speak, suspended in an atmosphere of eyes and mouths, of thighs and buttocks. A penis everywhere you turned; and breasts, too; and the lips of the vulva—both the labia majora and minora—there, too. When a couple reached an orgasm in the Mirror Room, it was many couples that reached an orgasm. It would be impossible for a man to lose his erection in that room, impossible for a woman to remain frigid. That room was a temple to love. *Thanks to*—stated the advertising brochure of Mônica's Place— *the magic of the mirrors.*

Such magic Elvira had tried to reproduce in her room. She had placed mirrors, six of them, on the walls and ceiling. But the reflecting surface was too small. The largest mirror probably measured no more than twenty-by-fifty centimeters. They would capture half a boob; or three toes; or a hairy rump; or one nut. An atmosphere conducive to love? None whatsoever, not in her place. Her clients found the presence of all those mirrors odd (in order to comb one's hair, one mirror is enough), and never for a moment did they suspect that the mirrors were there as traps to capture the fleeting bird of love. Anyway, they weren't the type of men who would enjoy looking at themselves while screwing; they'd think it was something for men who couldn't get it up, or for fairies. Rua Voluntários will always remain Rua Voluntários, Elvira would say with a sigh, and the Maipu will always be the Maipu, and I'll always be in this shitty life.

I said good-bye and slowly went down the stairs. For a long time I didn't go back to her. I would see her on the street, wave at her from a distance, and that was all.

At that time we had a housemaid, Sereni, a girl from a small town, very ugly she was, poor thing: rotten teeth, hair that was like chaff, and a stench that stifled you. But when I was feeling horny, she was there, and she didn't charge or ask for anything in return. Say that you love me, Paulo, she would implore me in a tearful voice as we lay in bed, and that was all. I love you, Sereni, I would say reluctantly. After school I would wait until Mother left for church, which she would do at six o'clock in the evening, and then I would steal into Sereni's room, located at the back of the house. My mother praying for her folks in Portugal, and I screwing Sereni—the whole thing made me feel guilty.

Benjamim would sometimes come with me. Not often; he didn't like Sereni. Besides, I think he missed Elvira. In our chats he often mentioned her. When he wasn't on about Jerusalem, of course.

ONE DAY, BENJAMIM WAS TELLING ME, I WAS WALKING ALONG
Rua Voluntários. I couldn't have been more than five years
old. . . . I had run away from my parents' store, and I was
wandering about the street. It started to rain, people were
running for shelter in the stores, in the bars. There was one
moment when I found myself all alone on the street, in the
heavy rain that was falling. Come inside, boy, people were
shouting at me, you'll get wet. I paid no attention to them. I
couldn't tear myself away from the cigarette butts, from the
scorched matchsticks, from the dried orange peels—from those
things that, you know, are considered garbage, but I was
concerned about them. How could I not have been concerned,
when the cigarette butts, soaked with water, were beginning
to disintegrate, when the rivulet that began to flow in the
gutter was already carrying the matchsticks toward the drain,
and from there, heaven knows where they would end. Nobody
worried about rescuing them.

I started to cry, Benjamim went on. Feeling sorry for the
rubbish, and sorry for myself, too, because it fell to me to
effect their rescue. Under the laughter and the taunting of the
bystanders I gathered together everything I could, the cigarette
butts, the matchsticks, the fruit peels, the empty cigarette packs,

55

then placed them carefully in the entrance hall of a hotel near
our store. A couple was then descending the stairs. This kid is
nuts, the man remarked to the woman. They went out
laughing, stepping on the objects, on those precious relics that I
had just rescued. Now you see, Paulo: Jerusalem . . .

Benjamim was telling me very personal things. I should have
been listening attentively, as a friend is supposed to; I should
have been looking at him with sympathy and understanding,
but I wasn't. Or rather, one of my eyes, yes, was gazing at
him with sympathy and understanding, but the other wasn't;
the other eye was far away, and yet not too far away: on the
mirror hanging on the wall in my bedroom.

We were in my bedroom, studying mathematics. The end-of-
the-year exams were approaching and we had, at best, only a
vague idea about the subject. The Pythagorean theorem meant
nothing to us, absolutely nothing; it didn't resonate in our
ears like a Beethoven symphony, perhaps because neither of us
had heard any Beethoven then. As for geometry . . . I look at
a rhombus, one of our classmates would say, and I see a vagina,
and that was that, as far as the rhombus was concerned.

We were studying math. Studying, in a manner of speaking.
Our books lay open before us, but at that moment Benjamim
was unbosoming himself to me while I sat looking at myself in
the mirror behind him.

What I saw didn't entirely displease me. Nowadays I'm fat
and balding . . . but at the age of sixteen I was a good-looking
lad. Dark eyes, black hair carefully combed back with a
forelock falling over the brow, a smile, slightly seductive,
slightly ironic, slightly childish, slightly sad. A shadow on my
upper lip. A few pimples, naturally, but nothing incurable.
Straight nose, unlike Benjamim's, that was irremediably hooked.
His hair, curly and unmanageable, was an indefinite color,
something like hay or camomile. And his pimples kept sprouting
ruthlessly, leaving huge craters behind after they finally
decided to heal. He was ugly, poor Benjamim. He would have a
hard time finding a girlfriend.

And would I? No. I knew I would be able to get one at will.
The girls on my street were already writing me notes; and in
my wallet, made of crocodile skin, I carried six three-by-four-

centimeter photos they had given me, inscribed with words
that ranged from nice to ardent. One Aninha wrote me poems;
Glória, the daughter of a neighbor, had even asked my
mother to persuade me to take her to a matinee movie at the
Imperial.

In those days, however, I was still not interested in girls.
Already almost interested, but not yet completely interested in
them. Benjamim and I had started frequenting the Maipu
again, and had resumed visiting Elvira, now cured of gonorrhea;
she had even insisted on showing us the clean bill of health she
had received from her doctor. And that's how it went: Elvira
as a routine, Sereni in an emergency. Girls? No, I wasn't
interested in them. However, should I become interested ...

Benjamim was now off again on Jerusalem. He was describing
the splendors of the golden city. He was quoting psalms. He
was talking about the girls of Jerusalem, maidens with big dark
eyes and black tresses. He was so moved that his voice
cracked.

There was a crack in the mirror, I suddenly realized. The
crack line could well be the bisector of the upper left triangle
of that rectangle. Was it really the bisector? Or was it the
hypotenuse? Or the secant? Or a meridian? I didn't know. I
didn't know beans about math.

Neither Jerusalem nor the Maipu. At that moment passing
the exam was all that mattered.

If we weren't doing well in math, it was mainly Benjamim's
fault, for he kept antagonizing the teacher, an unpleasant
little man with an aquiline nose and thin lips that never parted
in a smile. He always wore gold-rimmed glasses and a dark
suit, and always carried about an umbrella. His stealthy way of
entering the classroom without our noticing he was there had
earned him the nickname Shadow. Everybody hated him,
especially Benjamim, who thought the teacher discriminated
against him. He's an anti-Semite, Benjamim would say, he's
going to flunk me. Usually say, Benjamim underwent a
transformation in the Shadow's class. He would get up, challenge
the teacher, state that the subject being taught had nothing to

do with the curriculum. Every once in a while the Shadow
would expel Benjamim from the classroom. Sticking up for
him, I would walk out, too. And the two of us continued to fail
in the weekly quizzes.

   For several days the two of us had been trying in vain to
memorize theorems and formulas. All to no avail: there was no
way we could learn that stuff by heart. We came to the
conclusion that we were going to flunk the exam. Unless we
came up with some bright idea.
   We began to think of ways of cheating in the exam. Right
away we discarded the most obvious ones, such as writing the
formulas on scraps of paper, which we would take with us; the
Shadow knew this trick only too well. I thought of using a
small radio, with a transmitter and a receiver, which would be
great, except that we had no access to this kind of equipment.
Benjamim came up with a simpler method. He even tested it:
he got hold of a pair of dark eyeglasses, and on the lenses he
wrote the propositions of the main theorems. He then put on
the eyeglasses; on the outside, I verified, nothing could be
detected. And on the inside? Benjamim stood still, his mouth
hanging open as if he were ecstatic. Can you read anything? I
asked, hopeful. Sighing, he took off the glasses: No, he couldn't.
The letters were much too close to the eyes.
   As a matter of fact, we knew beforehand that any method of
cheating would be useless. The Shadow would keep us—his
enemies—under implacable surveillance. But even so, we continued
to think up plans, which became increasingly more fantastic.
We contemplated the possibility of getting the exam questions
from the Shadow himself, by resorting to various stratagems.
We considered using seduction: Elvira would meet him at the
door of the school, as if by chance, then lure him to her
room, where in the heat of passion she would wheedle both the
questions and the answers out of him. An interesting idea,
but with hardly any chances of being successful. The Shadow
would never go anywhere near a rendezvous on Rua
Voluntários. Unless he went wearing a disguise, like Doutor
Alfredo.

We consulted the Captain. Why don't you steal the questions? he suggested. We laughed; he was not amused. He was perfectly in earnest. On a table of the Maipu he penciled a plan of action. One night we would board a boat docked at Pier C-3 (the Captain offered to lend us his tugboat), and with our faces blackened with shoe polish, like commandos, we would disembark at Praia de Belas. We would don masks, make a raid on the Shadow's house, immobilize its residents—and guards, if any—at gunpoint, search the house, steal a few objects of little value to throw people off the scent, and, of course, copy the exam questions without attracting any suspicion. We would then make our escape just as quietly as we had come.

Benjamim and I remained silent. It's a good plan, I finally said; the only problem is that the teacher doesn't live in Praia de Belas.

"He doesn't?" said the Captain in disbelief. "But where does he live then?"

I didn't know for sure; perhaps in the Menino Deus neighborhood. But I was sure he didn't live in Praia de Belas.

The Captain was puzzled. So where in the world did I get the idea that the man lived in Praia de Belas? But even if he doesn't, he reasoned, we can still make good use of this plan. If you disembark at Praia de Belas, from there you can reach Menino Deus, which isn't too far away. You could crawl all the way there. . . .

We balked at the suggestion of crawling. But in the end, the idea of stealing the exam questions prevailed. There was really no other alternative. Benjamim was still reluctant, but I had already made up my mind, and eventually I won him over after mentioning instances of students who had stolen exam questions and later became good doctors, engineers, and other professionals. After he finally agreed to my plan, we then turned our attention to practical details. First of all, we would have to find out where the exam questions were kept. Knowing that the Shadow, a distrustful person, never brought anything to school with him, we concluded that he must keep them at home.

We had no idea where he lived. And without raising suspicions, we couldn't ask the school secretary for his address. I decided to follow him home.

I waited until he left the school building, then I tailed him. He boarded a Menino Deus streetcar. When the vehicle moved away, I ran for it, and then stood dangling from the balustrade on the rear platform. From there I could keep an eye on him without attracting his attention.

The Shadow got off at the end of the line. And so did I. Keeping a cautious distance, I followed him as he hurried away with mincing steps. He turned a corner, turned another one, then a third one. On a peaceful, tree-lined street, he came to a halt in front of an old house with faded paint. Taking a key out of his pocket, he unlocked the door and went in.

From behind a tree I watched the house. The Shadow was wary of burglars: he knew how to protect his household against them. There were grilles over the windows. A high gate equipped with iron pickets resembling medieval spears blocked the entrance to the driveway. To one side of the house was an empty lot covered with vegetation and mounds of garbage. Separating the house from this empty lot was a wall as high as the gate, with barbed wire and broken glass on the top. Through that wall I would gain access to the house.

It'll be a cinch, I said to Benjamim, child's play. It didn't seem all that easy to me, but I wanted to cheer him up. He was terrified. To steal exam questions is one thing, but to break into houses, that's a very different kettle of fish, he kept saying. Leave it to me, I said. All you have to do is to stay in the empty lot and be on the lookout. If you notice anything, don't worry about me, just whistle to me and then cut and run.

We fixed a date for the operation: a very auspicious Friday it was—Yom Kippur, the Day of Atonement. Nobody would notice the coincidence that both of us happened to be absent from school on the same day. As a Jew, Benjamim would be exempted from attending classes; and as for me, on the day before I would ask to be excused from class, claiming a medical appointment.

"Sounds fine," said Benjamim, "but . . ."

He was still wavering. I can't do something like that on a holy day, he mumbled. I lost my temper. So, take your holy day and shove it! I shouted. Go on, pray, and see if Jehovah will make you pass the exam. Okay, I'll go, he said.

* * *

Hidden around a corner, we saw the Shadow come out of
the house with his wife, a short, immensely fat woman. With a
wife like that, no wonder he's such a sourpuss, I whispered.
Benjamim laughed, constrained. He was trembling, all of a
sweat, but trying to disguise his fear.

After locking the front door of the house, the Shadow tested
the lock of the gate. Satisfied, he took his wife by the arm
and the two of them walked toward the streetcar stop. The
street was deserted.

Now, I said. We made a dash for empty lot, and hid
ourselves behind some bushes. I examined the wall again. It
was high but full of bumps and hollows that would help me
scale it. I took off my shoes. To my astonishment, so did
Benjamim. What for? I said, surprised. There's no need for you
to take off your shoes; you're staying here. He looked at me:
I'll stay here, yes. But if you happen to find yourself in a pickle,
I'll jump over the wall and lend you a hand.

Poor Benjamim. Frightened as he was, he did his best to put
on a bold front, maybe to prevent his fear from spreading to
me. A real friend, Benjamin was.

We shook hands; I got ready. I rolled up the legs of my
pants, took a deep breath, made a headlong dash for the wall,
then leaping at one of the iron rails that supported the barbed
wire, I hung on to it. With difficulty, and scraping myself
against the wall, I succeeded in raising myself; then warily, I
peered at the grounds.

I could see the driveway, onto which the windows on the
eastern side of the house opened. All the windows were
closed, and nobody in sight. I heaved a sigh of relief. Exerting
all my strength, I scrambled up the wall and gashed my hand
in the barbed wire. Even so, I jumped down and landed on the
cement floor. Without worrying about the wound, I tried to
peep through one of the windows.

As luck would have it, that particular room happened to be
the Shadow's study. There were shelves crammed with books,
a blackboard with geometrical figures and equations chalked on
it, a desk on which were several yellow envelopes. Even from
where I stood I could read what was written on them. The
examination questions! Oh boy, was I in luck!

The problem now was how to enter the house. Should I break
a windowpane, open the window from the inside, go in?
Walk around to the back? I hesitated.

"What are you doing here?"

What a fright I got! That feeling of the heart stopping, then
racing . . . I turned around.

No, there was no reason for panic. Gentle were the eyes fixed
on me, despite the glitter of irritation; and pleasant was the
face of the girl—for it was a girl, an adolescent, for sure, with
salient breasts—but anyhow, younger than me. And so pretty.
She had a round face, full lips, and beautiful hair falling over
her shoulders—I would have preferred that she wore it in
braids. It seemed incredible that such a gracious creature could
be the Shadow's daughter. And yet there was no doubt about
it; the same features, except that what was ugly in the Shadow
reappeared in her as beautiful, harmonious.

What are you doing here? she repeated. She wasn't startled;
no more than I was. I tried to dissemble. What a scare you
gave me, girl! Trying to speak in a casual tone, I said that I
had jumped over wall in search of a ball.

She looked around. There's no ball here, she said, now
suspicious. Then she saw my hand bleeding. You've hurt
yourself, she cried out, alarmed. It's nothing, just a scratch, I
said. Taking my hand, she examined it attentively (and now,
in close proximity, I could gaze at her face: beautiful), and
became alarmed. But it's a deep gash. She took me by the
arm. Come in, and I'll dress the wound. Leading me to the
back door, she showed me into the living room. I sat down
on a rattan sofa, under the portraits of ancestors with stern
expressions—was it their accusing eyes that I could feel on
the top of my head? She came back with gauze, a Band-Aid,
mercurochrome, and began to dress the wound. I could feel
her breath on me, her soft hair brushing over my arm. What's
your name? I asked, and my voice came out trembling, a
screech, almost. Maria Amélia, she said, applying the Band-Aid,
and yours? Ernesto, I replied, feeling myself blush. She didn't
notice; she was still busy dressing my wound. There you are,
she cried out, this will make the bleeding stop.

Expertly done, I said. She laughed: I have a knack for this

sort of thing, wouldn't you agree? I should study nursing. But
what I really like is singing. I'm going to be a singer, you
know. An opera singer. I've been taking lessons.

"At the Conservatory?" I was now feeling relaxed, at ease, I
had even forgotten that I was in the Shadow's house.

She shook her head.

"At home. I only study at home. The teacher comes here to
give me lessons. We have a piano in the front room."

She hesitated. "My father doesn't really like me to go out."

The Shadow, the unpleasant presence of the Shadow: the
key, the lock. The barbed wire.

"Father prefers to educate me in the old-fashioned way. He
doesn't allow me much freedom. Lina, my older sister, was
always having rows with my father. She ended up running
away, she now lives in São Paulo. But, you know, I don't
want to run away. After all, they are the parents God gave me,
I have to look after them."

For a few moments we sat side by side in silence—a silence
that disturbed me. I kept looking at her out of the corner of
my eye; and when our sideways glances met, it was electrifying.
I didn't know what to do. I had always considered myself
experienced in women, what with Elvira and all the rest of it,
but now ... There was a radio in a corner of the room, which
gave me an idea.

"Let's dance."

Bashful, she laughed, saying she didn't know how to dance—
how to sing, yes, but not how to dance.

"Come on, I'll teach you."

I turned on the radio and tried to find some romantic music.
To the sound of a bolero, we began to dance. You're pretty
good, I said, and she laughed, nervous, as I felt her small
breasts against my chest. Slowly I put my cheek against hers.
Watch out, Ernesto, she said, faltering, trying to push me away,
but I was already clasping her in my arms and kissing her,
and she, no longer resisting me, was kissing me, too.

Lying on his stomach in the empty lot, Benjamim had been
waiting, with his heart, he told me later, leaping in his chest.
Gradually, however, he calmed down. The hot sun had a

salutary, restful effect on him. He felt as if he were on a distant
beach, far from everything. He was no longer a transgressor,
an accomplice in a theft. In a abstracted and merry mood, he
lay gazing at the ants, which were busy walking back and
forth, transporting fragments of leaves along a trail; he watched
them skirt the clods of red, dried mud blocking their path.
Benjamim would have gladly spent hours there.

At that time: I, scaling the wall, cutting myself, bleeding; he,
watching the ants. But I, kissing, discovering LOVE; he,
watching the ants. I, living; he, looking at the ants. No wonder
he had the vision he had. After a while what he saw was no
longer ants on a trail. What he saw was a pass through rocky
mountains; a long column was advancing in the sun. At the
head were the scouts—dark, stocky men clad in simple loincloths,
moving swiftly, running along the trail, scaling the steep
mountainsides, scrutinizing the surrounding area from the top,
then climbing down to report back—*the coast is clear, no
enemy in sight*—to the commander of the troop. The soldiers:
one hundred in the vanguard, one hundred in the rearguard,
breastplates, spears, leather sandals pounding on the dusty path
to the sound of drums. Behind the soldiers came the slaves,
some stooping under the weight of the load they were
transporting, some carrying curtained litters—with concubines
inside. And finally, holding himself upright on his white horse,
his crown glittering in the sun, his dark eyes sparkling, his
black beard fluttering in the wind, none other than the king,
advancing, awesome, amid his army: Solomon.

It was Solomon's voice that Benjamin could hear at that
moment. And the monarch was far from being in a lyric
mood. It was not passages from the Song of Songs that he was
reciting. Actually, at first Benjamim couldn't understand the
words, spoken in Hebrew; they sounded far away, indistinct, as if
being received by an old radio with a great deal of static.
Finally, he could hear them loud and clear—*Lech l'Ierushalaim!*
Such was the command of the irate king: Benjamim was to
go to Jerusalem, pray in the Temple, and there expiate his
sins—the theft of the exam questions being the least serious of
them.

*   *   *

I don't know how long the two of us, Maria Amélia and I, sat there holding each other, without speaking. Hours, perhaps. Suddenly everything popped into my mind—Benjamim, the exam questions—and I jumped to my feet. Startled, she looked at me. What is it, Ernesto?

"I've just remembered that . . ." I began to explain, when I heard the sound of the key opening the front door.

Terrified, we stared at each other. Slip away, she said, which was exactly what I was going to do—but what about the exam questions? And the yellow envelope? It would be easy, all I had to do was to grab it as I cleared out.

No. I couldn't do it. It was no longer possible. Quickly kissing her once more, I tore out of the house, climbed up the wall with the swiftness of a cat, and jumped down onto the empty lot, where Benjamim lay prone on the ground, watching the ants.

They were making love, Solomon and the Queen of Sheba. Right there, before the entire entourage. They hadn't even bothered to hide themselves in a curtained litter. Why should they? He was the king. Her brown arms were clasping Solomon's naked torso. They moaned, they laughed.

"Scram!" I shouted. Bewildered, he jumped to his feet. I gave him a shove, the two of us took to our heels and ran for dear life down the street. We didn't stop until, exhausted, we reached the streetcar stop. Only then did we realize that we weren't wearing our shoes.

The day of the exam came. The Shadow handed out the questions. I didn't have a clue, I had absolutely no idea how to solve the problems. Benjamim, although he had stayed up all night studying, didn't seem to be faring any better. As for the Shadow, he kept a close watch on us. He kept looking at us with a peculiar expression—was it sarcasm, hostility, or melancholy?

I got up to hand in the exam paper. Wait here, will you? he said. I want to have a word with you and Benjamim.

Little by little the room emptied. Finally only the three of us remained. Closing the door, the Shadow turned to us.

"I've a present for you, boys. For you, Benjamim, and for you, *Ernesto*."

He removed a parcel from a valise. Even before I opened it—the Shadow was now smiling—I knew what it contained. Our shoes.

We both flunked the exam and we would have a second chance at the end of the summer vacation, but Benjamim chose not to avail himself of this opportunity. He decided to quit school and work in his parents' store. He told me again that he would like to study history, but in Jerusalem, etc.—the same old story.

As for me, I worked my ass off. I spent my vacation pounding the books; I didn't leave the house, not even to go to the Maipu or to a movie. I lost weight, my parents even became worried. No need to go overboard, they kept saying, after all, it's just an exam.

It wasn't just an exam. It was much more. It was the Shadow, it was my honor at stake in my situation with the Shadow. And it was Maria Amélia. Yes! I was in love. Among the math formulas I would write down her name. Among cones and spheres I would draw her face. And I would reshape triangles, even scalene triangles, into bleeding hearts pierced by arrows. Yes, I had it bad for her. Maria Amélia, I would murmur while embracing Sereni, who was surprised, poor soul, at my transports of passion. Maria Amélia. No other girl interested me. She's the one, I assured Benjamim, there's no doubt in my mind. He forced a smile and mumbled something I no longer remember. I couldn't keep Maria Amélia off my mind.

February came. I took the exam again. I passed. I just scraped through, but I passed.

On the day when the marks were given out, I went to see the Shadow at the school. Full of anxiety, and swallowing my

pride, I asked in a trembling voice for permission to see Maria
Amélia.

"On Wednesdays and Saturdays," he said dryly. "And at my
house."

And so I began to call on Maria Amélia every Wednesday and
Saturday night. We would sit talking, within sight of the
Shadow. Later he allowed us to go out together on Sundays.
We would go to a matinee movie at the Imperial. Despite the
watchful eyes of Maria Amélia's mother, who always chaperoned
us, I managed to hold her hand and steal a kiss in the dark.
We wanted so badly to become engaged, to get married. Say
that you love me, Paulo, Sereni would ask me, and I: All
right, Sereni, I love you. It was no longer difficult for me to say
so.

During that time I drifted away from Benjamim. We no
longer went to school together, and although we saw each other
almost daily, something had changed, something of significance:
I had a girlfriend, he didn't. I was happy, he wasn't. He wanted
to tell me about his troubles with his parents, with his
brother, but I was rather unwilling to listen. He wanted to talk
about Jerusalem, but I now found this kind of conversation
boring.

But I tried to be helpful. I thought of finding him a
girlfriend. I spoke to Maria Amélia. She had a cousin, who
would probably be suitable.... It was difficult. Benjamim was
ugly. Besides, he couldn't date a goy. Everything was so difficult.

There would be a moment, however, that was to unite us
again. A very important moment. Decisive, perhaps.

I NEVER GOT TO FINISH SENIOR HIGH SCHOOL, WHERE I WAS enrolled in the sciences program. I quit school, partly because of my unwillingness to continue my studies, partly because of my mother's illness. In July of 1955 she suffered her first hemoptysis, and after that she was in no condition to help my father anymore. When her condition worsened we had to place her in a sanatorium, and then things around here started to go downhill. Father and I would take turns at housecleaning, cooking, minding the bar. Both the Captain, who now came here every day, and Benjamim offered to give us a hand. But my father was much too proud to accept any help.

I hardly ever went to the Maipu and I didn't see much of Elvira. Once in a while I'd go with her to her room. She kept complaining: Just because you've got yourself a girlfriend, Paulo, you don't want me anymore. That's not true, Elvira, I'd say. But, yes, it was, it was because of Maria Amélia, of my girlfriend. I was afraid I would catch a disease from Elvira and pass it on to Maria Amélia. I felt responsible. I felt respectable.

Every Wednesday I would call on Maria Amélia. I had to arrive at eight o'clock sharp; if I showed up a few minutes early, the Shadow would pull the watch out of his vest pocket.

It seems to me, he would say in an acid tone, that you're champing at the bit, Ernesto.

Ernesto. That's how he called me when for some reason he wanted to antagonize me. *Ernesto*, or *honest Ernesto*. So, honest Ernesto, have you been busy working behind the counter at your father's bar? Or: What do you know, Ernesto, about the importance of being honest?

Dona Vitória treated me more kindly. She came from a traditional family in the city of Pelotas. An expert confectioner, she was always pressing her cream puffs on me and was genuinely moved by my compliments: No, not really, Paulo, I've lost my touch. I'm a mere shadow of the confectioner I used to be. (At the word *shadow*, it was all she could do to keep a straight face.)

The cream puffs were followed by an hour of artistic recreation. Dona Vitória would sit down at the piano, adjust the stool carefully, then strike the keyboard with determination: an aria from Verdi's *Aida*. Beside her, Maria Amélia, her eyes fixed on the ceiling, would be waiting for the moment to break into song—a moment that always touched me and gave me gooseflesh. She sang beautifully, Maria Amélia did. She still does.

At the end of the recital I would break into applause, naturally; the Shadow, however, would put a damper on my enthusiasm. You'll have to exert yourself more, he would say to his daughter; the high notes, in particular, could be better. Lina was excellent in the high notes, Dona Vitória would begin to say, but the Shadow would cut her short with a gesture.

An embittered man. He had been cheated out of his youth. His father, an accountant, after being indicted on a charge of embezzlement, spent years in jail.

"He didn't commit a crime. He made a mistake. But a mistake involving numbers is a crime. You don't play with numbers. Maybe that's why I've devoted myself to mathematics," he would conclude with a melancholy smile.

The Shadow didn't get along with the other teachers in the high school; according to him, his colleagues were always trying to hoodwink him. He knew that the students abhorred him.

"I know they call me the Shadow. I don't mind. Like the
Shadow, I know all about the evil that lurks in the human
heart."

Few friends. One of them was Doutor Alfredo, who sometimes
would drop by, bringing antisubversive literature. Closeting
themselves in the Shadow's study, they would talk at length.
This man is an example to all of us, the Shadow would say
after Doutor Alfredo had taken his leave. I steer clear of
politics, it's too dangerous in my opinion, but I must admit
that Doutor Alfredo, when defending his ideas, comes across as
an altruistic man.

It was from the Shadow that I learned that Doutor Alfredo
obtained funds for his organization from sympathizers, who
made donations to his cause. One of the most important had
been the Captain's father, who had even loaned Doutor
Alfredo a boat so that he could go on a campaign in the
interior. Did the Captain know that his family had such
connections? He had never broached the subject to us.

The cream puffs, the recital—they didn't engage my attention;
what I wanted was to be alone with Maria Amélia. At the
very most, though, the Shadow would allow her to see me out.
At the door we would exchange a quick kiss, and that was
all. I would return home to find Father in a state of despair.
Mother was becoming steadily worse. Death was slowly
drawing closer. In her delirium, she would talk about her village
in Portugal—which would grieve Father even more.

The Shadow would send her his regards, naturally; and
Dona Vitória, a plateful of assorted pastries; and Maria
Amélia, with tears streaming down her face, would say: I know
what you must be going through, Paulo, it's terrible, but no
matter what happens, I'll always be with you.

As it turned out, it was Benjamim who happened to be with
me on the day Mother died. The two of us were in the bar
when a friend of Father's, the owner of a wholesale business on
Rua Conceição, came in with a phone message he had
received from the hospital, requesting that we go there right
away. Father was just then returning from the bank, where he
had gone to arrange for a loan. We locked up the bar, then the

three of us—Father, Benjamim, and I—got into a cab and
headed for the hospital, a small, old, privately owned sanatorium
located in the district of Teresópolis. The owner, a sinister-
looking German doctor by the name of Schmidt, was waiting
for us at the entrance. It's the end, he lost no time saying, it's
the end. He then led us down a dark corridor to a room,
which Mother shared with two other patients. He asked
Father to go in.

"You boys wait outside."

We sat down on a wooden bench and watched the door in
front of us. A very tall door with panes, the kind of door
often seen in old houses. But up to a certain height—the height
of a grown-up man—the panes had been painted blue, which
prevented us from seeing what was going on inside the room.

Suddenly a hoarse, strangled scream. I made a dash for the
door. It was locked. Open it! I yelled. Open this fucking
door, I want to see my mother! They didn't open it. Distraught,
I began to jump up and down in an attempt to see through
the unpainted panes at the higher level of the door. And what I
saw—frozen images, jumbled-up snapshots—were to be the
last memories I have of my dying mother. One jump: wide-
open eyes, a tapering nose, an oxygen tube affixed to a
nostril with adhesive tape. Another jump: my mother trying to
lift herself up, the doctor restraining her with difficulty;
another jump: a nurse trying to give her an intravenous
injection; another jump: hemoptysis, the bed sheets stained
with blood; another jump: Father kissing Mother on the
forehead, a farewell kiss, it seemed; another jump: her
body already covered with a sheet, only the soles of her feet
visible.

"She's dead, Benjamim!" I cried out. "I think she's dead,
Benjamim."

Benjamim was standing at my side. Climb on my shoulders,
he said. He crouched; I mounted myself on his shoulders. He
was smaller and weaker than I was, but even so, he managed to
support me on his shoulders as he stood wobbling. Now, yes,
I could see everything. She was dead, all right, Mother was: the
nurse was rolling up the oxygen tube; the doctor was patting

Father's back. Silent, apathetic, the patient on the bed next to hers looked on. It was all over.

Benjamim set me down on the floor. I tried to say something; I couldn't. In tears, I clung to him. The door opened, my father stepped out, and there we stood, father and son, forlorn, not knowing what to do. Ships adrift.

LIFE BECAME VERY DIFFICULT: MY FATHER AND I, NOW ON OUR
own (Sereni, in tears, had left us, claiming I didn't love her
anymore), had to do the cooking, the laundry, the ironing, the
housecleaning, and on top of all that, to look after the Lusitania.
It was difficult, very difficult. Benjamim would try to cheer
me up. In vain—at times I was even rude to him. The fact is
that I didn't feel like talking to anyone, with the exception of
Maria Amélia, who in those days used to listen to me patiently.
It was only after our wedding that she started to gripe at me.

Then one day Benjamim stopped dropping by. Senhor Arão
felt it was his duty to give me an explanation. He came over
to see me, said that Benjamim was having problems, that they
had taken him to a specialist. He asked me to keep the
matter secret; he didn't want anyone on Rua Voluntários to
know that his son was seeing a psychiatrist. You know how it
is, Paulo, they'd soon start saying he's crazy. But you're a
friend, so I can confide in you.

Senhor Arão was in constant contact with the physician.
What he learned from the doctor, and from Benjamim
himself, appalled him. It's a problem with his mother, Paulo.
Jerusalem, those ideas of his, everything—it's because of his
mother. And Senhor Arão couldn't help feeling flabbergasted.

73

Frima, of all people, I'll be darned! Now, if it were because
of Nunho, that I could understand, Paulo. Nunho has always
been mean to his brother. But Frima! Look at her, Paulo, and
tell me: do you think that poor Frima is capable of causing her
son problems? A saint of a woman she is, Paulo!

And then Benjamim ran away. For the first time. It happened
in 1956, a year I remember well, for Israel was always in the
news then because of the Sinai campaign. I think that Benjamim
must have been deeply upset by the whole thing. Besides,
the medical treatment wasn't very successful, according to
Senhor Arão: Benjamim refused to accept the idea that he
had problems with his mother. He would miss appointments;
the doctor would have to phone to inquire after his
patient.

One morning Senhor Arão crossed the street running and
entered the bar, with a letter in his hand.

"Benjamim has run away, Paulo! Benjamim has run away!"

Devastated, he let himself fall upon a chair. The Captain,
who happened to be in the bar, rushed to him and proffered
him a glass of water. Read this, will you, said Senhor Arão in a
very feeble voice.

I took the letter and had a hard time deciphering Benjamim's
scrawl: *By the time you read this, I'll already be far away.*

There were several pages full of recriminations against his
parents: Benjamim accused them of misunderstanding him, of
having stifled his aspirations. His harshest words, of course, had
been saved for Nunho: they ranged from *wicked* to *criminal*,
with *mucker, gangster, thief* in between. Finally Benjamim
described in idyllic terms the life he intended to lead, a life
devoted to studies and meditation. He was willing to face all
the risks of both the journey and the new life (he would have
to live in a territory controlled by Jordan), but, he added, the
risks didn't matter; the important thing was the fact that he
was answering the call of Jerusalem.

"The call of Jerusalem!" Senhor Arão kept crying out. "The
call of Jerusalem is important! All right, so it is. I couldn't

agree more. But what about the call of his parents? Isn't it as
important? Tell me, Paulo: parents are important, are they
not? Or are parents nothing? Is Arão nothing? Is Frima
nothing? Tell me, Paulo, is this how you treat your own
father? Was this how you treated your dear mother, may she
rest in peace? Would you leave your parents? Tell me, Paulo,
is Jerusalem more important than one's parents?"

I tried to calm him down. Don't worry, I said, he'll be back
in a day or two, you'll see, sir. But in fact I wasn't all that
sure: Benjamim had taken all his clothes and—what was
worse—his parents' savings, which they, distrustful of banks,
kept in a vase under the portrait of the grandparents.

"He cleaned us out!" wailed Senhor Arão. "He took everything
Paulo. We were left destitute. Ungrateful son!"

He was shouting so loudly that passersby were stopping on
the street to see what the commotion in the bar was all about.
Close the doors, Father said. I closed one of the doors and was
about to close the other when Nunho walked in, as usual
dressed to the teeth in a sleek alpaca suit, a flowered shirt, a
white necktie. Everybody paused, including Senhor Arão.
Nunho slowly walked up to his father, the dark lenses of his
eyeglasses reflecting back the lights of bar. He took his father
by the arm.

"Let's go, Father. Let's go home."

"Ah, Nunho," moaned the old man. "Have you heard what
that bandit has done to us?"

"Yeah," said Nunho in his harsh, threatening voice. "But you
and Mom shouldn't worry. I'll teach him a lesson, that idiot. I
already have someone looking after this matter. My partner, Big
Dog, is already taking action."

Now that was bad news, for this Big Dog, a hunk of a man
with a bulldog's face, happened to be even worse than
Nunho. He was involved not only in contraband but in drug
trafficking as well. A bandit; rumor had it that he had once
dumped two stiffs into the waters of Alemoa Inlet. At that
moment I feared for my friend; although I would miss Benjamim,
I was hoping he would never come back—or that he would
come back only after things had cooled down.

*   *   *

But Benjamim did come back, and sooner than expected. To be precise: six days later.

Late one night I woke to the sound of tapping on my bedroom window. Groggy with sleep, I got up to open it, and lo and behold, there stood Benjamim, hunching his shoulders against the drizzle that was falling.

"Benjamim! For heavens sake, man, where have you been?" I said, at once astounded and happy. I asked him to come in.

But he refused. "You come out," he said. "Let's go for a walk, and I'll tell you everything."

I threw on my clothes and, careful not to make any noise, went out. Deeply moved, Benjamim hugged me without saying anything. Then, as we walked along the deserted streets, he told me about what had happened.

He hadn't gotten anywhere near Jerusalem. Or Israel. He had never left Brazil; in São Paulo he had stayed at a cheap rooming house near the bus station—and there he had been robbed while asleep.

"They took everything, Paulo. I was left with nothing but the clothes I had on. In order to come back to Porto Alegre, I had to hitch a ride with a truck driver, a very kindly man. If he hadn't paid for my meals, I would have gone hungry."

He fell silent for a moment. His face, wet with rain—or was it tears?—filled me with such great pity that I couldn't bear to look at him. It'll turn out all right, I murmured. One day you'll get there, Benjamim.

"To Jerusalem?" He was not transfigured; he looked like a visionary, a prophet. "One day I'll get there, Paulo. Even if it's only to touch the Wall. Even if it's only to die there."

He asked me to accompany him to his parents' home. It's just that, he said, I'm afraid, you know, they'll raise the roof, but if you're there with me, they'll show restraint.

They didn't. As soon as Benjamim rang the doorbell and shouted, "Don't be alarmed, it's me, I'm back," they opened the door—Senhor Arão in pajamas, Dona Frima in a nightgown—and threw themselves upon their son, crying, laughing, hugging, kissing, and recriminating him, too.

"You murderer! You bandit! You've almost killed us, you good-for-nothing!"

They insisted that I go in. "Don't stand there in the rain, Paulo, you'll catch your death." Dona Frima made tea; we sat eating cookies and chatting. Senhor Arão told us stories about Europe; Dona Frima kept correcting him—the two of them would laugh. Benjamim would smile. Nunho didn't turn up. Everything was fine: taking my leave, I returned home.

It must have been around that time that Father began to change. It wasn't anything sudden; he had been depressed ever since Mother died. But it was then that he first became slovenly in his dress; he stopped wearing a necktie and he no longer carried about the emblem of African chieftaincy. There were always stains on his clothes, he dropped cigarette ashes about, he didn't flush the toilet. And he talked to himself. Well, not to himself—to Mother. Her spirit visits me every Thursday, he confided to me. Do you know why, Paulo? Because we were married on a Thursday; that's why she pays me a visit on this day.

A difficult phase. Maria Amélia was a great comfort to me; I had really lost my heart to her. Had it been up to me, by that time we would have been engaged, if not married; the Shadow, however, wouldn't hear about it.

"There's plenty of time, Paulo. Let the girl study singing for a while longer. There's plenty of time, you're both very young."

I was now working all day long: Father had stopped coming to the bar. "What for?" he would say. "To make more money? I'm not interested in money, Paulo. Or in anything else."

He would wander downtown, without any clear destination in mind. Or he would go to the wharf, where he would spend hours staring at the ships.

I was forced to run the business all by myself. I hired a cook, who wasn't very good, and a waitress, who was even worse. Before the month was over I had to fire both of them. The bar was dirty; I was fined several times by the health inspectors. The old clientele, consisting mostly of merchants whom Father knew well, gradually stopped coming. Only my friends would come: Benjamim, Elvira, the Captain. And Orígenes, who always came together with Benjamim.

And yet, oh, land of glory,
if I have never seen thy essence
why do I remember thee in thy absence?

—Camoëns

THE TWO OF THEM, BENJAMIM AND ORÍGENES, WOULD TALK
at length as they sat at a table in the bar, Benjamim drinking
beer, Orígenes sipping at his glass of milk (he never drank
any alcohol, at least not in public). They would exchange
confidences in a low voice, which would intrigue me. What in
the world did they have so much to talk about? Orígenes is a
deeply spiritual man, Benjamim would assure me. He didn't
look the spiritual type at all. Stocky, bald-headed, talkative, and
full of tics—always blinking his eyes, pulling at his left
earlobe, shrugging his shoulders—the man looked more like a
traveling salesman, which incidentally he used to be before
becoming a priest of the sect the Lord's Companions—the only
priest the sect had in Porto Alegre, in Rio Grande do Sul,
and, as far as he knew, in the entire Brazilian land.

"This man"—and Benjamim would proudly point to him—
"has wandered through the Valley of Death, Paulo. This man
has suffered, this man has wept, this man has sweated blood."

"Not really," Orígenes would say, modest. "It wasn't as bad
as all that."

"Of course it was!" Benjamim would cry out. "Of course it
was! You wandered through the Valley of Death! Until you
finally found the way!"

"Well, that's quite true," Orígenes would admit. "I did find the way." Then, picking up the cue:

"What was I before? A rascally traveling salesman, always on the road. I worked, of course, I sold my wares—costume jewelry, fabrics—without ever wondering about life's fundamental questions. Who we are, where we are going, whether there's life after death—I never wondered about any of it. I was partial to booze, to cards; I used to frequent all the cabarets in the towns along the Argentinian and Uruguayan borders. My life changed when I met the Reverend Jonathan Foster in the town of São Lourenço. The hotel was full, so I had to share a room with him. This gringo is going to get my goat, I thought when I saw that red-haired behemoth of a man. But then we started to talk— and let me tell you, at that moment I saw the light. The story of the Reverend Jonathan, my friends, was truly inspiring."

(The story of the Reverend Jonathan. Born in 1908, in a small town in the southern United States. His father, a small farmer, an alcoholic. His mother, a submissive woman, has to endure beatings from her husband, for she is considered impure. Eight brothers. The oldest, Francis, seeks refuge in the attic. There, amid the ancient uniforms and the rusty swords of the Confederates, he begins to have his first visions: angels materialize before him and ask him to found a new religion, whose followers are to build a Christian kingdom in Jerusalem. Enraptured, Francis outlines his initial plans, then over dinner, he discloses them to his family. Widespread sneering. All his brothers, with the exception of Jonathan, who decides to fully support Francis, laugh so much that one of them even chokes on a piece of chicken. Francis's new visions amplify the initial plan. It's no longer a matter of conquering just Jerusalem; Palestine and the entire world are now included in the plan. It's essential that all human beings become *the Lord's Companions*. And then Francis dies. As he tries to embrace an angel leaving through the window in the attic, Francis falls down from a height of twelve meters and fractures his skull. His brothers say it isn't any big loss, but Jonathan vows to devote

his life to propagating Francis's ideas. Before embarking on
his mission, however, he is seduced by the wife of a farmer in
the vicinity; for months he surrenders himself to the joys of
sex, his initial design completely forgotten. Then he is drafted
into the army. He gets involved in a brawl, is expelled from
the army, then drifts across the United States, at times working
as a book salesman, at times a taxidriver or a waiter—taking
on a variety of jobs. Nothing works out; it's as if he were under
a curse. One night, as he lies drunk in a gutter in Memphis,
Tennessee, the ghost of Francis appears to him. This time he is
inexorable, saying that Jonathan *has to* establish the Lord's
Kingdom on Earth right away. *Patagonia*, the ghost murmurs
before vanishing.)

"But even so, Jonathan wasn't convinced," Orígenes would
continue. "Instead of beginning to preach to the incredulous, he
went to Baton Rouge, in Louisiana. While strolling on the
beach, he saw a whale in the distance behaving in an odd way.
The whale kept jumping up into the air, diving, jumping up
again. Jonathan, who was rather boozy, dismissed the incident
as unimportant. Then all of a sudden the whale was at his
side; it opened its mouth wide and swallowed Jonathan. . . ."
    "But isn't this the story of Jonah, from the Bible?" I would
ask. Reproachful, Benjamim would look at me, as if to say,
How dare you interrupt the man?
    "It bears some resemblance to it," Orígenes would admit to a
serious tone. "But as I was saying, the whale swallowed
Jonathan and took him to a freighter bound for Patagonia. The
whale didn't desert Jonathan, though: it followed him from a
distance throughout the course of that voyage, and of many
others as well. The whale, Paulo, was an emissary of the
Lord, chosen by Him to work with the leader of our sect, do
you understand? But returning to Jonathan: in Patagonia he
changed an entire tribe of Araucanian Indians into the Lord's
Companions. Afterward he went to Bariloche, a resort town
in Argentina, where for a while he earned a living by selling
souvenirs to tourists. While there, he wrote *The Book of
Revelations*, which contains all the fundamentals of our religion,

including procedures for administering baptism, for holding
religious services, for raising money—everything. It was in
Bariloche that he also met Irmgard, the daughter of German
immigrants; at first a loyal companion, she soon turned out to
be an ambitious woman. She wanted Jonathan to convert, as
quickly as possible, millions of people. She wanted magnificent
temples; she wanted to live in palaces. Before the reverend
could carry out his mission in Bariloche, she had talked him
into moving to Buenos Aires. There they rented a house in
the district of Caminito, where they set up the seat of the
church. It wasn't difficult to convert the tango dancers when
they were drunk and disgusted with the world, but as soon as
they sobered up, they would forget their promises and go
back to the cabarets in the Boca neighborhood, there to trip the
light fantastic. In addition to those frustrations, Jonathan had
to put up with a lot of insolence on the part of Irmgard, who
was possessed—it was now patent to him—by the devil.
There was no man capable of satisfying her; she kept accusing
the reverend of being impotent. One night, feeling desolate,
Jonathan was walking along the banks of the Riachuelo River
when there was a disturbance in the dark waters, and lo and
behold, guess who heaved in sight right before him? The whale,
his loyal whale! There was no hesitation. As soon as the
whale opened its mouth, Jonathan threw himself into it. The
whale took him just a short distance away and deposited him
on the other bank of the river—but Jonathan understood the
message: that very night he got on a train bound for a town
on the Argentinian border. And there I met him; at the right
moment. I had been going through a difficult phase in my
life, I had broken off a a relationship with a woman, I was
leading a dissolute life, gambling like crazy and boozing up.
In Jonathan I found myself again. On that very night I was
converted, and he baptized me by pouring a whole bottle of
milk upon my head. At dawn he appointed me as priest of our
church in Porto Alegre and neighboring municipalities. He
showed me *The Book of Revelations*, but didn't go into any
details about how I should perform the religious ceremonies.
He just said that the Lord would demand a great deal of
astuteness on my part. As a matter of fact, he gave me a

concrete example: In the morning we went to the hotel lobby
for breakfast. The place is crowded, and Jonathan walks up to
a man and asks him for his watch. The man, rather stunned,
complies with Jonathan's request; Jonathan drops the watch
into a small bag, then throws it on the floor and stamps on it.
The man, furious, draws his gun—but then Jonathan takes a
meat turnover from the counter, breaks it open—and behold!
Inside is the watch, all in one piece and in working order. A
trick or a miracle? It doesn't matter. What matters, Jonathan
later said, is to attract believers by any means. I'll have one of
your meat turnovers, Paulo."

I would serve him a meat turnover; he would pick up the
story again.

"Too bad, as I said earlier, that we didn't get a chance to talk
more. On the following day Jonathan left town. He left me a
note, saying that Francis's ghost had called him and that he was
on his way to Jerusalem."

Orígenes would take a sip of milk.

"I'm sure, my friends, that the whale came for him. I'm sure
that on that night Jonathan stood on the edge of the lake,
alone in the rain and the wind. And I know that at one
moment the whale, having left the south, the sea, was
drawing near. It came to the shore of the lake, opened its huge
mouth; Jonathan went in, and was gone. The rest you know.
I came to Porto Alegre. set up the temple, began to work."

The temple of the Lord's Companions was in an old
warehouse near the bus station. Orígenes liked the location
because it was right on the route taken by many of the
newcomers to the capital city: farmhands who came in search of
a job, girls who hoped to find employment as housemaids,
young boys who had run away from home, as well as the sick
and the crippled who came for medical treatment.

The temple itself was a long, poorly lit hall, damp and cold.
On the wall at the far end hung a crude wooden cross and a
sign Orígenes himself had made: REPENT, it said. A few chairs,
a few wooden benches, five or six collection boxes on the side
walls, and nothing else. A temple should be a simple, ascetic

place, Orígenes would say, but in fact, even if he had wanted
to decorate the hall in a more suitable way, he wouldn't have
the money for the improvements. Besides, there wouldn't be
anyone to appreciate them. Except for the huge rats scurrying
to and fro, the place was as good as deserted. The only
faithful follower was the hawker Peep-Less. At nightfall,
when people no longer stopped to buy his elixir, Peep-Less
would go to the temple. He would enter quietly, and after
leaving the small table, the suitcase with the merchandise, and
the valise with Pascoal and Catarina in a corner, he would kneel
down and pray, with sighs and moans rising in profusion
from his hollowed chest. When he was finished with his
prayers, he would have a quick chat with Orígenes, reminisce
nostalgically about his life on the frontier, and take his leave.
Orígenes could then lock up, for nobody else was going to
drop in. Notwithstanding the sign on the door offering services
(PRAYERS. COMFORT TO THE DISTRESSED. FAITH HEALING);
notwithstanding the pamphlets that he had a boy hand out
every once in a while at the bus station (*Would you like to find
out about the path to truth?*); notwithstanding the presence of
Orígenes himself at the door, where he would stand, friendly,
smiling, and even importunate (*Come in, son! It won't cost you
anything!*); notwithstanding all his efforts, services were not
conducted for absolute lack of attendance. So there was nothing
else for Orígenes to do but to lock up the temple and go
home, where Irmgard would be waiting for him. This was
another amazing thing in Orígenes's life. About the sudden
appearance of Jonathan's former wife, he would tell us the
following.

"One day Irmgard showed up in Porto Alegre, bag and
baggage. Jonathan himself had given her my address—to this
day I don't know why. She complained about Jonathan, said he
had deserted her, and asked if she could stay with me. Well,
at that time I was living in the temple, then newly established,
by the way; it didn't seem proper for me to have a woman
staying there, the churchgoers would right away think of some
hanky-panky going on between us. But she insisted, saying
she would help me, she would do the cleaning, she would
decorate the walls and the altars, she would even get together

a group of the Lord's Lady Companions and together they
would make a drive among the local merchants to raise
money for our church. She seemed so understanding, so
convincing, that I ended up giving in to her. Well, let me tell
you, already on the second night she crawled in bed with
me—and she's been bossing me around ever since. The
religious services should be held in this way, baptisms should be
administered in that way. Until finally I came to the conclusion
that there was no room in the sect for both of us. I'm awfully
sorry, Irmgard, but you'll have to go. I thought she'd just
pack and leave—but instead, Paulo, know what she did? She
pounced on me. We fought, Paulo, we grappled with each
other—and I'm not ashamed to say that I was defeated. She
wrestled me to the ground, I was overpowered. Promise you'll
marry me! she kept screaming. I promised: I'll perform the
wedding ceremony today, without delay, I said, almost choking.
Not here! she yelled. In a registry office, you swindler! In a
registry office! And so we were married. But don't think that
my hardships are over, Paulo. She nags me all the time; she
accuses me of being incompetent, of being unable to recruit
any followers; she says that Isidoro, a fellow who founded a sect
in the district of Cavalhada, is already a millionare, and that
I'm just marking time. And she comes up with such absurd
demands, she wants me to change the name of our sect to
God's Squirrels, which she claims was its original name. Squirrels,
Paulo! Okay, they're nice, diligent little creatures; one could
even mount an advertising campaign with this theme: posters
showing squirrels carrying crosses and the caption—*Let's
collect virtues for eternity just as squirrels collect nuts for the
winter*—but, frankly, Paulo, who in Brazil knows anything
about squirrels? They're exotic little creatures, Paulo. Now, rats,
yes; folks know them well. I've even thought of a splinter
sect, the Lord's Little Rats, or the Lord's Mice, maybe with
Mickey as the symbol to give it an aura of American
efficiency. But Irmgard dislikes rats."

Orígenes would fall silent for a moment, then go on again.

"True, she's a good woman, a good cook, and she does the
laundry, keeps the temple clean, and I must say her complaints
are valid, but what am I supposed to do, Paulo? If only I could

have one look at *The Book of Revelations*. This book holds the
key to all the problems in our religion, Paulo, to every single
problem. It would make my work so much easier."

"And what about Jonathan?" I would ask. With a shrug,
Orígenes would reply that he had never heard from him
again. A moment later, however, with a glitter in his eyes and a
hopeful tone in his voice, he would say:

"Have you heard about this American who's been preaching
in Jerusalem? Near the Wailing Wall? Hmm? Have you,
Paulo? About this American who shows a watch to the crowd
and says that the minutes still left to humankind are running
out? Well, Paulo, I have, and I'm sure it's none other than my
friend, my priest—Jonathan. A watch; that's typical of him.
Yes, it must be Jonathan. One of these days I'll go to Jerusalem
and look him up. And I'll return with the book, you bet I
will. One day I'll extract watches from your meat turnovers,
Paulo! Silver watches!"

(Once, in a frenzy of enthusiasm, Orígenes was unable to
control himself. He removed his wristwatch, threw it on the
floor, stamped on it; then, snatching a meat turnover from the
counter, he ripped it open. It contained, like all the other
meat turnovers, nothing but minced meat and hard-boiled egg.
Perplexed, he stood staring in turn at the meat turnover, at
the shattered watch. And now, he kept murmuring, how am I
going to explain this to Irmgard?)

I must have spoken to Irmgard no more than three or four
times. A robust, blond Valkyrie with grayish eyes. Talking, she
didn't seem the harridan of Orígenes's description. On the
contrary, she had grounds for complaining about the Lord's
Companions. In her Portuguese mixed with Spanish, which
her German accent made ever harder to follow, she would say
to me: I'm fed up with the whole lot. They keep promising
the Kingdom of Heaven and a life of ease.... A life of ease?
Hard work, that's what it is. I'm sick and tired of sweeping
the temple, of cooking, of doing the laundry. A life of ease? I
haven't had it yet. Wait until the believers start coming,
Orígenes says to me. Believers, my foot. The only one who ever

comes is this weird Peep-Less, and he doesn't have a pot to
piss in. Ah, and the rats. You wouldn't believe the rats in this
temple, Paulo! Twice, already, they've attacked me while I
was sweeping the floor.

A pause, after which she would continue, her voice quivering
with contained indignation.

"Not that I have anything against rodents, Paulo. My father
used to raise squirrels in Bariloche. But those were cute,
sensitive, delicate little creatures, who would eat out of our
hands. Early in the morning they'd come into my bed and
run to and fro over me. It felt so nice, their tiny little paws ...
I love squirrels. Now rats are something else, they're disgusting.
I can't understand why there are so many rats in Porto Alegre,
in such a civilized, European-like city. These repulsive creatures
must come from the slums. And they seem to have a marked
preference for the temple, I wonder why. There are never any
leftovers around here, Paulo, I can assure you."

Another pause, and then in a trembling, tearful voice: "I
even dream of rats, Paulo. Of the rats' heaven; gold-winged
rat-angels in white gowns, playing tiny harps. Rat-saints. Eleven
thousand virgin she-rats. Sitting on the throne, the King of
the Rats, a crown on each of his seven heads. The worst part is
that the doorman-rat never allows me in this heaven. He
drives me out, I fall into space, sink into the earth—and find
myself in the rats' hell. I'm tortured by rat-demons. They
throw me into caldrons—if only there were boiling oil inside!—
but no, there are rats inside, millions of them, rubbing
themselves against me, biting me, pissing on my wounds. Sheer
horror. Do you think I deserve this, Paulo?"

Then, wiping a tear: "No, I don't. I've already been through
a lot because of these two scoundrels. The first one lured me
to his sect—which he treacherously called the Lord's Squirrels—
Companions came later—seduced me on the pretext that he
was fulfilling a divine design, then ran away with the whale,
leaving me high and dry. The second one is a loafer, a dud.

"But I'll teach Orígenes a lesson," she would conclude,
raising an enormous fist. "I've beaten the hell out of many an
Araucanian Indian, and Orígenes is not any better than any of
those Indians. He'll have to deal with me if he doesn't get

himself straightened out. It's a promise, Paulo, and I don't have
to swear an oath on any Book of Revelations. I tell you,
Orígenes had better watch it because one of these days I'll
square accounts with him. On that day it would be better for
him to show a clean pair of heels, to flee to some distant place.
To Jerusalem, where he can join that other scoundrel. Because,
I tell you, on the day of reckoning, Orígenes won't get a chance
to flee. No, he won't."

Poor Orígenes, he did try hard. He even tried to convert us
to his sect. As for me, I wasted no time setting the record
straight: I'm terribly sorry, Orígenes, but running the bar is a
lot of work, and I have a family to look after; there's no way I
can assume any other responsibilities. The Captain, without
mincing words, said he had no time to waste on such bullshit.
Elvira also refused to join the sect, but she was more polite,
and claimed that since one of her brothers was a priest, it
would be impossible for her to give up Catholicism.

"But you have my sympathy," she added.

Kind, gentle Elvira. Remarkable in bed, even though she was
beginning to go to seed. In those years—1963, 1964—I still
frequented her place; I was already married to Maria Amélia,
but my wife was no longer the graceful teenager I had once
met. Thanks to her own meat turnovers and to Dona Vitória's
rich desserts—coconut puddings, cream caramels, meringues,
ladyfingers with cream filling—which she kept bringing us,
Maria Amélia had changed into a fat, irascible matron, the
mother of two whining sons. We lived with Father on Rua
Comendador Coruja, which only made things more difficult.
My father, then old and sick, disliked his daughter-in-law's
cooking, and he couldn't stand the children's noise. After his
death in 1965, the Shadow and Dona Vitória started to visit us
more often, which also didn't improve matters any. They
came all the way from Menino Deus (a district where the city
barons used to live, as the Shadow never failed to recall): he,
with his umbrella; she, with a Pyrex bowl of assorted desserts.
Every time they came, I always managed to leave the house
with the excuse that I had work to do in the bar. I knew that

they discussed me behind my back; the Shadow would say I
was incompetent, whereas Dona Vitória would accuse me of
having prevented her daughter from becoming an opera
singer. Even Lina, the sister who had run away from home,
kept writing from São Paulo, where she worked as a secretary
in a big company, to rebuke Maria Amélia for letting her
husband control her. *So typical of you Porto Alegre women,
you're fit only to be housewives. No São Paulo woman would ever
give up her career on account of her husband's bar.*

No, life with Maria Amélia wasn't easy. We often argued;
and in bed—in bed, she wasn't all that great. For solace, I
turned to Elvira. Who, incidentally, also had problems of her
own: she was then living with Big Dog, Nunho's friend. The
pimp kept all her money, forced her to put up with Doutor
Alfredo's kinkiness. After the military coup of April 1964,
Doutor Alfredo stepped up his precautionary measures. More
thoroughly than ever before, he would ransack the bedroom for
bombs. He suspected that Elvira might have connections with
subversive or vindictive types. Watch out, Elvira, he kept
warning her, I always stay on top of things. That I can see,
Elvira would mutter. I'll run away one of these days, Paulo, I
swear to God I will, she would assure me. I'll go back to the
farm.

But she stayed on. She was resigned to her situation, and she
even liked Big Dog. Actually her problem had nothing to do
with the gigolo. What worried her most, what kept her awake
at night, was the possibility of her family finding out that she
didn't own a bar, as she wrote in her letters, in which she gave
them the address of the Lusitania as her own. It seemed a
remote threat. Neither her parents nor the brothers who
worked on the farm ever came to visit her. As for the two
brothers who were priests—well, the younger one, a diabetic,
had died after a prolonged fast; the older one, Francisco, was
still living in Jerusalem, where he ran a hostel for pilgrims.
Once in a while he sent Elvira a postcard, which she kissed
reverently. He was the brother whom Elvira least expected—
and most feared—to see. And yet it was this very brother who
turned up in Porto Alegre.

*   *   *

One day a telegram from abroad was delivered to me at
the bar: it was for Elvira. Right away I thought it could only be
bad news. And indeed: no sooner had Elvira finished reading
it than she dropped the piece of paper, raised her hands to her
head, and let out a cry.

"He's coming here, Paulo!"

He, who? I asked. Your brother, the priest? Yes, him, she
groaned, Francisco, the priest! Coming all the way from
Jerusalem to visit me, Paulo! And he's arriving tomorrow!

Terrified, she clung to me. And now, Paulo? What am I
going to do, Paulo? Take it easy, I said, trying to free myself,
we'll think of something. But at that moment my mind was a
complete blank.

However, the Captain and I finally cooked up a plan. Our
idea was to put a scenario into effect during the priest's
two-day stay in Porto Alegre before he left for the interior to
visit the rest of his family. Elvira would be the proprietress of
the Lusitania, and I the manager. She didn't quite like the idea.
Isn't it a sin to lie to a holy man? she asked Orígenes. To the
best of my knowledge, it is not, replied Orígenes. It's a white
lie; all religions make allowances for it. What surprised us,
however, was Benjamim's reaction. I don't think it's funny at
all, he said when, laughing, I told him about our plan. You're
mocking a man who sacrificed his life to his faith, a man who
went to Jerusalem—what's funny about it? Disconcerted, I
was at a loss for words. But even Elvira began to think that our
plan was the best solution.

Father Francisco arrived, and there was nothing of the
martyr about him: tall, fat, with a broad, red face open in a
smile that revealed his gold teeth; he looked more like a farmer
pleased with his harvest, with life in general. Elvira had
picked him up at the airport; he came into the bar, greeted me
with his beautiful baritone voice, looked around, said that the
establishment wasn't too bad, although it was a bit dirty, with
lots of flies about—for which I apologized. We were
understaffed, it was hard for me to keep the place clean. Elvira,
decorously dressed in a dark outfit, with just a touch of
makeup, was great in her role as bar owner, but she couldn't
control her anxiety. When her brother asked her about

invoicing and billing, she looked at me, terrified. I came to her
rescue: Dona Elvira isn't quite up-to-date on such things,
Father; she looks after bank matters, business contracts, that's
her department, whereas I take care of running the business.
Excuse me if I seem to be meddling sir, said the priest, but it's
just that I'm in a similar line of business, did you know? I
manage a hostel for pilgrims in Jerusalem.

Then, as he started to tell us some amusing anecdotes about
pilgrims, Benjamim came in. We were apprehensive—Elvira,
myself, and also the Captain, Orígenes, and Peep-Less, who
were sitting together at a table, looking on. But Benjamim
conducted himself well. He chatted with the priest—about
Jerusalem, naturally. He asked him about the Wailing Wall,
about the Tower of David. The priest replied courteously but
without the degree of emotion that Benjamim had expected.
He was disappointed. They weren't soul mates. Then, saying
good-bye, Benjamim went back to his store.

Another alarming incident was still in store for us that day.
Unexpectedly Big Dog put in an appearance. He didn't
approve of Elvira's sober attire.

"What's that for, woman? Are you now aping some highfalutin
dame or what? Go and change those fucking clothes."

Quick action was essential. Grabbing Big Dog by the arm, I
took him outside. He was foaming with anger: The cow, why
isn't she working? What is she now, a regular faggot's moll?
And he a priest, too!

A bright idea struck me. Not so loud, I said, he's no priest,
he's a cop in disguise, he's been asking an awful lot of
questions about Nunho, about you, and we've been trying to
put him off the track. Big Dog looked at me in disbelief. A
cop? Come on, disguised as a priest? That's right, I said. Scram,
Big Dog, I urged him, he's itching to send you to the
slammer. Big Dog hesitated. He looked at the priest, then at
me; finally he went away.

On the following day the priest left for the interior. In the
evening Elvira came over and thanked me profusely. We
drank a toast to our cleverness.

"Didn't I look pretty in that outfit?" she asked, with a glint
in her eye. "Listen, if I weren't a hooker ..."

She fell silent and stood staring out at the street, lost in thought.

Night was falling. Night was drawing near and there we were: myself, washing glasses; Elvira, leaning her elbows on the counter; the Captain, sitting at a table by himself; Orígenes and Benjamim together at another table; Peep-Less by himself at another table. Benjamim was talking about the Wailing Wall; Orígenes kept sighing: The Wall, yes, people hold it in reverence; if only I could transform my temple into a kind of Wall. Millenniums, my dear friend, Benjamim said in a restrained voice, it'll take you millenniums for that. Millenniums, muttered Peep-Less, already quite soused, what do you guys want with millenniums? Enjoy life now; look, there's Elvira giving you the come-on.

Elvira smiled and went to the door. Rua Voluntários was beginning to fill up with people. I must be trotting along now, she said. Doutor Alfredo must be waiting for me; Big Dog will kill me if I'm late. You must get rid of that pimp, said the Captain, he's a bandit, Elvira. I know, she said, you think I don't know that I should cut and run, Captain? Only too well. And one of these days I'll pack and leave for the farm. You guys wait and see.

It was all bluff. Elvira knew she lacked the courage to leave. And the truth of the matter was that Big Dog was fond of her. He had even promised to marry her—that is, if he could pull off a certain deal. But don't you slacken off, Elvira, he would warn her. Keep on working, I need a lot of capital for this enterprise I have in mind.

Elvira would go back to her room, Peep-Less would go home, Orígenes would go to his temple, and the Captain would fall asleep, his head on the table.

"See you later, my folks are waiting for me," Benjamim would say. He would walk across the street and enter his store. At peace with himself, or so it seemed.

NOW, IN RETROSPECT, IT SEEMS TO ME THAT BENJAMIM HAD
about five peaceful years—from 1962 to 1967. Maybe he didn't
feel all that peaceful in 1962 or in 1963, but there's no doubt
that he felt peaceful in 1964—a year I remember well because it
was marked by restlessness, not just on Rua Voluntários, of
course, but throughout the country as well; Benjamim, however,
seemed oblivious to what was happening in the country. He
continued to work in his parents' store, he continued to call out
to customers on the street; he would come regularly to the
bar for a beer; and in the evenings he would either go to a
movie or stay home immersed in his history books. His
parents insisted that he go out, that he go dancing, that he go
to parties, hoping that he would meet a nice girl and get
married, that he wouldn't turn into a weird bachelor, or into a
scoundrel like Nunho. But Benjamim wasn't interested in
finding a girlfriend. He remained faithful to Elvira, whom he
visited once or twice a week.

When Benjamim felt too anxious, he would go to his
psychiatrist and return with a prescription for tranquilizers.
He still had problems, Senhor Arão often confided to me.

Problems? Yes. In 1967, you bet. In the second half of the
year, to be more precise. It is easy for me to remember: It

was after the Six-Day War. Throughout the conflict in the
Middle East, Benjamim was at a high pitch of excitement,
listening to the news all day long, and he even attended to the
customers while holding his battery radio to his ear. After the
war ended he fell into a depression. He was no longer calling
out to the customers walking along Rua Voluntários with his
former zest; he was no longer shouting "it's cheaper here" in
that tone of voice in which the aggressiveness of the salesman
mixed with the bitterness of the frustrated historian. "Here,"
was all he said now. "Here!"—spoken through a raucous
megaphone, another symptom that something must be wrong
with him: he had always despised the megaphones of the
shopkeepers on Rua Voluntários. If shouting is what it takes to
sell, I'll shout with the voice that God gave me; if Peep-Less
can do it, so can I, he would say.

Yes, Benjamim was having problems then. And yet we never
imagined that he was on the verge of dropping everything
and running away.

One morning I opened the bar to find on the worn-out
tiled floor an envelope containing Benjamim's letter. I opened
it. Again the familiar scrawl, again the outpouring of grievances,
again the accusations. And again, Jerusalem: *Now that I can
finally live there,* he wrote, *nothing will prevent me from
fulfilling my destiny.*

I sighed, walked across the street, went into his store. His old
folks were there, quite beside themselves. Senhor Arão rushed
toward me: Benjamim has done it again. What will become of
him, Paulo? What will become of us? I tried to calm them
down: Don't worry, Benjamim knows what he's doing. But
Dona Frima couldn't resign herself to the fact that her son
had walked off without saying anything to them; he just left at
dawn like that, leaving a note behind: his parents were not to
worry, he had to follow his own path. Paulo will explain
everything to you, Benjamim ended his letter.

Me? But did I know anything about it?

(Yes, I knew. More than I thought I did; I knew about the
whole thing. Not that my knowledge would have made any
difference then, of course, but the fact is that I knew.)

Under the circumstances I would have to lie, and so I lied. I

told them that Benjamim hadn't been feeling well lately, that
he had been nervous, so he had decided to travel in order to
relax.

"To relax?" burst out Senhor Arão, at once perplexed and
incensed. "What do you mean, to relax? To relax just like
that, without a word to us, is this then the way to relax?"

I did my best to calm them down. I assured them that
Benjamim wouldn't do anything rash, that he would be back
soon.

And indeed, he did come back. This time, too, he never
went beyond São Paulo. He wasn't robbed, but he couldn't
travel abroad: he had no passport, so he had to apply for one.
While waiting for his application to go through the proper
channels, he got married.

It was all very sudden, and even Benjamim had been taken
by surprise: I never once thought that this could ever happen
to me, he later told us, beaming.

Three or four days after his arrival in São Paulo, Benjamim,
impatient at having to wait for his passport, goes for a walk in
Bom Retiro. The streets of that neighborhood remind him of
Rua Voluntários; he is homesick, and for the first time he
questions himself: Why do I have to go to Jerusalem? Why
has this idea taken hold of my mind? Why this hang-up on
Jerusalem? I don't even know if Jerusalem exists!

Suddenly he catches a glimpse of a young woman inside a
store. Jewish, obviously: it is perhaps her red hair, or perhaps
her nostalgic gaze, lost in the distance, that makes him notice
her. He goes in. On the pretext of inquiring after the price of
cretonne, he approaches her. They talk. Small talk: the weather
in Porto Alegre and in São Paulo, the amount of rainfall, and
so on. Why don't you have lunch now, Sula? says the store
owner, a fat old woman who looks a lot like Dona Frima;
she is the young woman's aunt. Benjamim is bold enough to ask
Sula to have lunch with him. They go to a nearby Yiddish
restaurant. Looking over the menu, they discover that marinated

fish is their favorite dish. They laugh. She has beautiful teeth.
A twenty-three-year-old orphan, she lives with her uncle and
aunt, who own the store. No, she doesn't particularly like to
look after the counter. But what else is there? She quit school;
she had no other skills.

Like Benjamim, she, too, feels lonely. Like Benjamim, she,
too, dreams of Jerusalem. Soul mates.

She decides to take the rest of the day off. I'll pretend I'm
not feeling well, she says, laughing. They stroll about the city,
go to a movie, have dinner at a small Italian restaurant,
and—to cap a perfect day—go dancing at a nightclub. Tyros,
these two dancers. While one moves to a bolero rhythm, the
other moves to a samba rhythm; while one dances to a rock
rhythm, the other dances to a tango rhythm. Sula trips: Benjamim,
laughing, steadies her. They stand gazing at each other for
a long time—the tenderness, the fascination growing by the
second until, on an impulse, they kiss. They kiss. A romantic
tune now envelops them, but they are not dancing: embraced,
they stand in the middle of the dance floor while couples
slide by in the semidarkness. They are in love. Without effort,
without embarrassment, Benjamim, happy, makes a simple
suggestion. Why not spend the rest of the night together?
Happy, she accepts the suggestion.

In the morning they go to Guarujá, a nearby seaside resort,
and have a picnic. And it's there, as they lie on their stomachs
on the sandy beach, looking at the sea, that Benjamim proposes
marriage to her. She laughs, looks serious, laughs again, then
breaks into tears. Yes, she will marry him, she believes in fate;
as soon as she saw him, she knew he was going to be the man
in her life.

They return to São Paulo to talk to her uncle and aunt, who,
suspicious and hurt because Sula has spent the night away
from home, want to know more about this young man from
Porto Alegre, about this Benjamim, who is in such a hurry to
marry a girl he has barely met. Benjamim explains himself, tells
them about his family—making, of course, no reference to
Nunho—shows them photographs. The uncle and the aunt, still
reluctant, try to play for time and suggest a period of
engagement first, but the lovers won't budge on this issue. On

that very day Benjamim phones the agent he hired to
expedite his passport application. Your passport is almost ready,
I'll bring it to you tomorrow, the man promises. What
passport? I'm not interested in any passport, says Benjamim. I
don't want to travel, I want to get married. Could you get me
the proper papers? Astounded, the agent says he certainly can.

"He must think I'm crazy," Benjamim says to Sula, "and he's
right, I'm crazy, crazy about you."

On the following day they go to a registry office, are
married—the religious wedding ceremony will take place later—
and leave for Porto Alegre.

We were delighted to hear about Benjamim's marriage, even
Elvira, who was losing a good client. Big Dog isn't going
to like it, she confided to me, apprehensively. She shrugged.
Well, that's his tough luck, what's important is that Benjamim
is happy. And then, smiling, she reasoned: Actually, who said
Benjamim won't visit me anymore? You visit me, Paulo;
Benjamim can visit me, too. Married or not, I continue to like
you guys.

We decided to throw a party for Benjamim and Sula.
Orígenes, braving Irmgard's fury, offered us the temple, and I
would supply food and beverages. As for entertainment, leave it
to me, said the Captain, who played the mouth organ.
Peep-Less volunteered to sing gaucho songs.

On a Saturday night we gathered at the temple. Senhor Arão
showed up, but Dona Frima had refused to come—we knew
it was because of Elvira. As a matter of fact, Maria Amélia
stayed home, too, pleading a headache—but I knew the real
reason was the presence of Elvira.

About ten o'clock in the evening Benjamim and Sula arrived.
She was a nice person. Not pretty, but then Benjamim was
nothing to write home about, either. The important thing was
that Benjamim looked cheerful, and cheerfulness was what he
really needed, for until then he had had more than his fair
share of sadness. It was Sula who, after the toasts, the songs, and
the first signs of ebbing conversation, suggested a game to
liven up the party: It's called The Road to Jerusalem, she said.

Following her instructions, we arranged the chairs in a circle, with their backs turned to the center; then to the sound of a march played by the Captain, we trotted around the chairs. Suddenly the Captain stopped playing, we sat down, one of us eliminated—Senhor Arão. We removed one chair, resumed our trotting, the music stopped, and this time Irmgard was out. Finally only Elvira and I remained running around the single chair to the frenetic tune the Captain was playing. As soon as the music stopped, Elvira pushed me away and sat down: I won, I won, she cried.

"What is it that you won?" boomed a voice from the door. "Tell me, you whore, what did you win?"

It was Big Dog, fuming. Walking up to Elvira, he grabbed her by the arm: On a Saturday night, with Rua Voluntários packed with people, and Doutor Alfredo looking for you, and here you are playing games, you bitch! I thought Big Dog had gone too far and decided to challenge the bully: Listen, Big Dog, it's none of my business but— Elvira interrupted me: Take it easy, Paulo. Then with a beseeching smile: It's okay, really. Big Dog is quite right. I should be working. Good night, folks.

She said good-bye to Sula.

"It was nice to meet you. Take good care of Benjamim, he deserves it."

They invited us to the religious wedding ceremony, which would be held at a synagogue in the district of Bom Fim. We decided we wouldn't go so as not to embarrass them, but Benjamim wouldn't hear of it: You're my friends! And you, Paulo, you're like a brother to me. More of a brother than Nunho has ever been, Paulo. It took me a long time to convince him: We're your friends, sure, Benjamim, but your friends from Rua Voluntários, not your friends from Bom Fim.

As far back as I can remember, Benjamim had never been as happy as he was in those days. He exuded joy; he enthused over his plans. He was going to expand the store, renew the stock, hire interior decorators. When he stood on the street attacking shoppers, his vendor's cry could be heard all the way from Praça Parobé to the railroad station.

"Here, my friends! Here, it's cheaper, here, it's better! The gentleman there in a cap, come in, sir, and pick and choose. It's right here, friend, you can't go wrong!"

I think Benjamim must have lived happily for a good two years. His cheerfulness only came to an end when Samir arrived.

BENJAMIM BEGAN TO HATE SAMIR EVEN BEFORE HE HAD EVER
met him. It all began when the owner of the store next door to
his sold his business and moved to the interior. Benjamim
had been waiting for such an opportunity to expand his
business. He was thinking of renting the premises. He went
to the real estate agency and came back furious. The place had
already been rented to one Samir, Benjamim said, annoyed.
To an Arab, Paulo. And I'll bet he's an anti-Semite, too. Don't
worry, I said to cheer him up. You don't really need the extra
space. And as for your new neighbor, he won't compete with
you; there's room for everybody. You're both merchants, and
eventually you'll come to an understanding. And maybe—I
raised the possibility—the two of you will form a partnership.
But Benjamim wasn't sold on my idea; with a scowl on his face,
he left the bar.

A few days later the façade of the vacant store was getting a
fresh coat of paint. Look at that color, isn't it hideous?
Benjamim complained, and he was right. It was a deep blue
verging on purple. The store signs annoyed him even more.
They advertised clothing articles for men, women, and children—
exactly what Benjamim carried in his store. Nothing enraged
him as much, though, as the name of the store: New Jerusalem.

He's got no right, he would clamor in the bar. We—the
Captain and I—tried to point out to him that the man had the
right to choose any name he wanted for his establishment.
But it's disrespectful, Benjamim would protest, to name a store
after Jerusalem. I can't accept it, I'm going to write a letter to
the newspaper.

   This does not bode well, remarked the Captain after Benjamim
left. Orígenes capitalized on the opportunity to proselytize,
but it was only a halfhearted effort: If people loved each other,
if everybody was the Lord's companion, such things wouldn't
happen. As for Elvira, she had no opinion about the matter, but
she made a prediction. The Arab? A new client, very likely. I
just hope, she said with a sigh, he'll pay for my services without
any hassles.

   We were all curious to see this Samir, the new neighbor.
Finally he appeared: one morning there he stood at the door
of his store, waiting for customers to arrive. A short, swarthy
man with a black mustache, still young in spite of his graying
hair. A Levantine, as my father would have said, a Saracen.

   As soon as I opened the bar, he came over, and after
studying the menu, he ordered a turnover and coffee.
Apologizing for his broken Portuguese, he explained he hadn't
been long in Brazil. He had left Jerusalem soon after the
Six-Day War.

   (Jerusalem—so that explained the name of the store. I was
far from being pleased. It was one more reason Benjamim
would have to fight with his neighbor.)

   Samir praised the meat turnover—the best he had ever
tasted—then told me that before he moved to Porto Alegre
he had lived in São Paulo for two years. He was doing well
there, making good money, leading an easy life, when suddenly
somebody tried to implicate him in a murder.

   "Didn't you read about it in the papers? A very serious
matter, pal. The courts cleared me of any wrongdoing, but I
decided to get the hell out of São Paulo. I was a marked man
there, know what I mean? A marked man. So I came to
Porto Alegre together with my brother."

   A murder, well, that seemed a bad omen, but Samir had

already changed the subject and was asking me about the
business situation on Rua Voluntários, about the volume of
business in the bar, in the other stores.

The truth of the matter is that the man was pleasant; he
struck up a conversation with the Captain, who had just then
walked in. The two of them chatted about ships, and much to
the delight of the Captain, Samir was an attentive listener.
When Orígenes came in, Samir introduced himself and expressed
an interest in the temple, promising to promote the Lord's
Companions among his acquaintances. As long as you send
customers over to me, Samir added, laughing. He nodded at
Elvira, who was coming in at that moment, and offered her a
beer.

And suddenly, standing at the door was a gray shadowy
figure silhouetted against the gray light of the winter morning,
the fog enveloping it like an aura. It was Benjamim. They
looked at each other, Benjamim and Samir. They looked at
each other and it was already an act of confrontation. The
tension: I could feel it in my neck, and in the Captain's
clenched fist, and in Elvira's partly open mouth, and in Peep-
Less's fixed gaze. I could feel the tension in the iridescent
bubble that appeared on the lip of the bottle of beer, and on the
shell of the meat turnover, and even on the surface of the
mirrors, of the tabletops. At that moment I wouldn't have been
surprised if a mirror had smashed to bits, revealing, not the
cracked wall behind it, but a black hole, the entrance to an
endless tunnel. I wouldn't have been surprised if the marble
top of a table had split open, releasing a red carnation or a
tongue of fire. I wouldn't have been surprised if the humidity
then saturating the air (ninety percent that morning, according
to the radio) had condensed into one single gigantic tear-
shaped drop suspended between the high ceiling of the bar and
its rather grimy floor; or worse, if this tear had become an
eyeball, Cyclops eye floating in the air, the dilated pupil
reflecting the Maltese crosses of the caravels painted on the
wall. And as for the caravels themselves, I wouldn't have
been surprised to see them sail across the air in the direction
of the river, and from there, already in the water, head for

the lake, for the sea, for Africa, and finally homeward to
Portugal.

Benjamim and Samir, and the space between them teeming
with invisible presences: souls in limbo, small demons, a few
angels, some evil spirits, fluids in general. What strange creatures
they were, this Benjamim, this Samir. Strange creatures who
had come from strange lands. It was something contagious.
Gradually everything here in the bar, people and things,
began to acquire a weird appearance. I was overcome by anger
and suddenly I felt like screaming: Get the hell out of here,
you fanatical partisans, you infidels, go back to your countries
and leave me alone: I belong to Porto Alegre, to the Navegantes
streetcar, to Our Lady of the Rosary Church, to Caminho Novo,
to Praça Parobé, to the plane trees in Redenção Park, to the
Provincial Bank, to the General Hospital, to the islands of the
Guaiba River, to the Shrine of Our Lady of Gloria, to Alto
da Bronze. This healthy anger, this holy wrath made me react;
exerting all my strength before the spell could ensnare us,
before we were lost forever, I succeeded in finding my tongue
again and I screamed in a voice that, albeit weak and
screechy, was the voice of a human being, of Brazilian, of a free
citizen of Porto Alegre.

"Benjamim!"

And presto, everything was back to normal: the beer bubble
burst, the Captain made a salute, Elvira broke into a smile.
Orígenes heaved a sigh, the mirror once again reflected normal
images, Samir took a bite at the meat turnover he was
holding in his hand and from the inside came no repulsive
worm or exotic insect; neither did any poisonous vapor swirl
out: judging by the crumbs on Samir's mustache, that meat
turnover contained, like all the others, nothing but minced
meat and hard-boiled egg. Benjamim walked in, no longer a
Jewish warlock with a goat's face, but just the friend of my
childhood, the companion of my adventures.

I introduced him to Samir. It was soon over. They exchanged
a few trivial remarks and Benjamim took his leave. Samir
stayed on for a while longer; he talked about soccer, said he
would have to choose a local team to root for, then he, too,
left.

*   *   *

Samir would talk to me about Jerusalem. But it wasn't the same as Benjamim talking about Jerusalem.

There was no quavering in Samir's voice, no magic in his words. His descriptions lacked vividness; his Jerusalem was a city just like any other, with lanes that, at the very most, I was able to imagine as being rather like the streets in our Lower City—somewhat narrower perhaps, more winding, more mysterious, with eyes peering from behind shutters, and the occasional cloaked figure or veiled woman walking by. What Samir liked best, though, was to reminisce about his childhood, so similar to our own childhood here in Porto Alegre, with the same kind of games. Games that Samir had to give up early in life in order to help his father.

"We had a souvenir store that catered to tourists. It wasn't big, just a one-door hole in the Old City, but enough for us to make a living. We sold souvenirs to the followers of the three religions; yes, to Jews, too; we never had anything against them, they were good customers. But my father disliked Copts. You know, we're Arabs but Christians. We attended the Christian church regularly; we had nothing to do with the Koran, the mosques, the recorded voice of the muezzin calling the hour of prayers, the praying on one's knees, and the beating of one's head on the floor while turned to Mecca. All of this was alien to us; we were Christians, followers of the Maronite denomination. My father was an ardent defender of his faith—and an enemy of all Copts. Copts, he used to say, are treacherous. They have the key to the door of certain temples in their possession and they won't let anybody in. Copts will kiss you, then stab you in the back; Copts will laugh with you while cursing you in their hearts. Copts are liars. Copts are betrayers. Don't even mention Copts to me, my father would say, unless you want to ruin my day. Poor Father, a kindly man, except that he had this fixation on Copts."

Samir would fall silent for a moment and then continue.

"We had an easy life in Jerusalem. Then the war broke out and the city fell into the hands of the Jews. My father, a proud man, decided to leave. From now on, he said, Arabs will have to work for Jews as waiters, as construction workers,

and I won't put up with this situation; this is something worthy
of the Copts, who betrayed their principles. We closed down
the business and sold part of our stock, keeping the more
valuable items, which we packed in suitcases, for my father
intended to set up shop in Jordan. And so the entire family—my
parents, my three brothers, and myself—left Jerusalem. Together
with a crowd of refugees, we walked across the Allenby Bridge
over the Jordan River. Before we reached the other bank, my
father, gripped by sudden despair, wanted to return to
Jerusalem—and it was a melee: my father fighting against
that human current, and me trying to dissuade him, when
suddenly the suitcase I was carrying opened, spilling its entire
contents into the water. Crucifixes, they were—very pretty,
made of wood, with a white plastic Christ, a crown of thorns,
droplets of blood—the whole kit and kaboodle. And they were
now floating in the water. But not for long: the Christs were
hollow, and as the water seeped through the wounds, they sank.
My father said nothing, but he was obviously filled with despair.
My brothers tried to comfort him: It's water from the Jordan
River, holy water. Then my father slapped me in the face. I
said nothing and swallowed the insult, but I decided that I had
had it, that we would have to go our separate ways. As it turned
out, my parents and two of my brothers went to a refugee
camp, a filthy place, much worse than any slum here; my
younger brother and I came to Brazil. I resolved to make a lot
of money, Paulo. So that nobody would ever slap me in the
face again, know what I mean? So that nobody would ever kick
me out again."

   Making money became quite an obsession with Samir. And
he was determined to reach his goal as soon as possible. As a
merchant, he was far more enterprising than Bejamim: he
enticed all and sundry into working for him. For a small
payment, he hired Peep-Less, then temporarily out of work
(his goods had been confiscated by the city inspectors), to cry
the wares at the door of his store, where he was to stand
wearing an Arabic turban. To the cabbies stationed in the taxi
stands in the vicinity Samir offered a twenty-percent discount

on any cash purchase they made at his store if they were willing
to distribute advertising leaflets among their fares. He promised
the same discount to Elvira and other women as well, provided
that they sent customers to him.

It was with a jaundiced eye that Benjamim watched such
goings-on. He would say nothing—as a matter of fact, after
Samir became a regular at the bar, he rarely put in an
appearance—but it was obvoius that he was about to blow his
top. The Palestinian, too, was openly hostile to Benjamim—and
to Jews in general. It's because of them that I had to leave my
hometown. They've probably torn down our house. It was
near that Wall, and all the houses in that vicinity were razed.

The rest of us tried not to meddle in this matter; we wanted
to be on good terms with both of them. Elvira, in particular,
was thrilled when she learned that Samir was from Jerusalem.
She asked if he happened to know her brother, Father
Francisco, the one who ran a hostel for pilgrims. Yes, indeed,
Samir knew him, and he knew the Reverend Jonathan, too
(an outstanding figure, very popular in Jerusalem), which left
Orígenes deeply moved and hopeful that one day he would
see his master again.

As for me, I didn't buy those stories. I suspected that Samir
made up much of what he told us. But there was no reason
why I should speak my mind to him. He was a good customer,
a pleasant gabber, and it was all the same to me whether he
told lies or not. If I deplored this situation at all, it was only on
account of Benjamim: three months after the Palestinian's
arrival, he was completly unhinged. This man is a terrorist,
Benjamim told me in confidence. He would cite signs of
sabotage: mislabeled merchandise, men's underpants stored in
boxes that should have contained shirts, socks with holes in
them, a dead mouse in the pocket of a pea jacket. But how, I
would ask, could Samir possibly have placed a dead mouse in
the pocket of a pea jacket in your store? But Benjamim
wouldn't give in; he always had explanations for everything:
an agent of Samir's, posing as a customer. Besides, it's possible
to train a rat so that it will get into the pocket of a pea
jacket, where it will stay until it dies. He would invoke

Irmgard's testimony: She knows what rats are capable of,
Paulo. All it takes is a crafty person to handle them right, and
they'll commit horrors.

He kept complaining that Samir was an unfair competitor
who was always underselling him, that Samir would stand on
the sidewalk to steer shoppers into his own store. When
municipal workers started digging a hole in front of his store,
Benjamim came running into the bar: This son of a bitch is now
even pulling strings at City Hall to get me, Paulo.

The excavation, however, gave him an idea. One afternoon
he shouted to me to go over to his store; then taking me to
the back, he unfolded a role of translucent tracing paper on the
table. Any idea what this is? he asked with an air of mystery.

It looked like a blueprint. It is a blueprint, he confirmed.
And he added: of *his* store. He smiled: This here in red is a
system of pipes that I'll be installing myself ... secretly, of
course. It starts here at the back of his store, and ends here at
that small gate he has.

"Do you know what these pipes will carry, Paulo?"

I had no idea.

"Gas." he said, triumphant. "Hydrosulfuric gas, Paulo. A gas
with a nauseating stink of rotten eggs, strong enough to drive
customers away."

I tried to dissuade him from going ahead with his plan. In
vain: he installed the piping, and even tested it once. He had
to give up the whole idea. The gas flowed back into his own
store. Senhor Arão and Dona Frima complained: He's crazy,
completely out of his mind, not even his psychiatrist can handle
him anymore.

They asked me to intervene. So one night Maria Amélia and
I went to the apartment that Benjamim had rented on Rua
Farrapos after his wedding. Sula, looking vexed and tearful,
opened the door.

"He locked himself up in the bedroom at noon and hasn't
come out since. See if you can make him come out, Paulo."

The apartment was in complete disarray, with clothes and
books strewn everywhere. In a corner was the miniature
model of Jerusalem, surrounded by lit candles.

I went to the bedroom and knocked on the door. "It's me—Paulo. Open the door, Benjamim."

There was no reply.

I persisted: "Open the door, Benjamim."

I heard a heavy shuffling of feet followed by the noise of the key turning in the lock.

"Count until ten, then come in," he said in such a strange voice that I could hardly recognize it. I did as he told me, counted to ten, then opened the door.

Benjamim was nowhere to be seen. I peered under the bed, behind the grubby curtains: nothing. Suddenly the door of the closet flung open, and with a savage howl Benjamim sprung out.

"You're finished, you terrorist!" he shouted.

I stepped back. It was a fearful sight. Benjamim was wearing old army fatigues (undoubtedly bought at a secondhand store), combat boots, an ammunition belt from which hung guns and knives, and bandoliers across his chest. He was wielding a rifle, which he then showed to me with pride.

"Automatic. The best in the market."

But what's all this? I asked, alarmed. He smiled. Sinister: War is war, Paulo. I'll get him, by hook or by crook.

He took off his uniform and put it together with the weapons in an old suitcase, which he then locked. Sula mustn't know about this, he said to me in confidence. Neither Sula nor anyone else. Only you, Paulo ... But then, you I can trust.

I couldn't get over my shock. What do you intend to do with this arsenal? He looked at me, serious: I'm ready for whatever may come.

He told me he had been taking karate lessons. But he wasn't too keen on the martial arts: Firearms, that's what I'm really good at.

This would have to stop. Benjamim's deterioration was obvious: he was losing weight fast, he looked wan, there were dark circles under his eyes—and the delirious glitter in his eyes was foreboding.

I decided to play the role of mediator, I kept going back and forth between Benjamim's and Samir's stores. I would listen to them, I would reason with them. The Jew was more stubborn, more upset. Every day Benjamim had a new story to tell me; sometimes it was about Muhammad and his *believe or perish*, sometimes about the women forced to wear veils, or about the Africans, whom the Moslems had enslaved.

"You people also had problems with the Moslems, Paulo."

You people were, of course, my Portugese ancestors. But I wouldn't let myself be indoctrinated: Samir isn't a Moselm, I would reason, he's a Maronite Christian. I don't care what he is, he would say. I don't like him. The very thought that while we're here talking, he's right next door doing business, or counting money, or scheming, or laughing, or belching makes me want to puke, Paulo; the very thought is loathsome, it fills me with a hatred you can't even imagine.

Then looking at me sadly: "If only I could get rid of this hatred, Paulo. Well, I just can't, it's stronger than me. It's a mission, do you understand? A mission that I must carry out. Just as the prophets had a mission, so do I."

A mission—that's what made everything so difficult, that's what irritated me no end, this thing he had about Jerusalem. There were other Jews on Rua Voluntários who were also interested in Israel, who helped its cause, who went visiting there and came back all excited. And yet they continued to lead normal lives, without causing any problems. I don't like Arabs, one of those Jews once said to me, but then I don't like goyim either; I know it's an aversion, a hang-up of mine, my psychiatrist has already told me so; but just because I dislike them, it doesn't mean I want to pick up a fight with them.

A sensible man. Why did Benjamim have to be different? Why couldn't he be reasonable and accept things?

Samir was less complicated. He disliked his neighbor, and that was that. And he would rather not talk about it; he would change the subject, tell a joke, laugh. But the situation between the two of them was far from being a laughing matter, as it was made clear to me sometime later, not by Samir, but by his younger brother, a melancholy young man

with a squint in one of his eyes, which gave him an appearance
of not being all there. One day when I dropped in, Samir and
his brother happened to be eating lunch at a small table behind
the counter. With a knife, each brother was taking from a
can something resembling a white paste, which they spread on
slices of rye bread. They were eating ravenously. Suddenly an
argument broke out. Red with anger, Samir rose to his feet,
shouted something I didn't understand, and walked out. His
brother fixed his good eye, brimming with tears, on me: He's
mean, he said. Samir's mean, Benjamim had better watch out.
Then he began to sing a long, slow song in Arabic, and all the
while he was watching me. Ill at ease, I didn't know what to
do, whether to leave or stay and listen, whether to applaud or
remain silent. I was rescued by the arrival of a customer—but
my misgivings grew worse. I was beginning to think that not
even Solomon, the wise king, would have been able to find a
solution to this feud.

Elvira told me that Nunho was in town. I decided I would
look him up: he was a scheming man, and even though
Benjamim disliked him, they were brothers, and Nunho might
perhaps give me some suggestions about Benjamim's feud with
Samir.

I went to the hotel where he was staying—it was on Rua
Farrapos, a short distance from Rua Voluntários. I knocked
on the door of his room. Come in, said a hoarse voice. I went
in, and there he was in his underpants, lying in bed with a
beautiful blonde—naked, she was—but the fact didn't seem to
faze either of them. Get lost, Nunho said to her, I have to
talk to my friend. But where am I supposed to go? the young
woman asked. Lock yourself up in the bathroom, said Nunho,
throw yourself into the toilet bowl, or jump out the window. I
don't care, as long as you make yourself scarce. With a sigh
the blonde got out of bed, went to the bathroom, and closed the
door behind her. Stupid broad, muttered Nunho, and then
asked me to sit down.

I sat down and outlined the situation. He listened in an

abstract way, seemingly more interested in his manicured
fingernails, which he was examining with a creased forehead.
My brother is just hopeless, Nunho said when I finished. So
what are we going to do about it? I asked.

"What are we going to do about it?" Reaching for the glass of
whiskey on the night table, Nunho took a good swig. "What
can we do? My brother is nuts; the other guy is a prick, so I
gather. I know the type well. So what can we do . . . ?"

From the bathroom came the muffled voice of the blonde:
Can I come out now, love?

Stay there and shut up, shouted Nunho.

Then turning to me: "Listen, pal, I don't really want to be
drawn into this feud. I don't want to have anything to do
with my brother. However, I could ask Big Dog to take care of
the Arab."

No, it's not the case, I hastened to say. I think the situation
can be solved without violence: perhaps we could come up
with a few other ideas. Nunho laughed: Ideas are not my forte.
Now, if it's a question of roughing someone up—especially if
he happens to be an Arab—you can count on me.

I stood up. I'm going out, too, Nunho said. I waited for him
to get dressed—which took him a long time. At the door I
asked about the girl.

"What girl?"

"The one in the bathroom."

"Ah!" he laughed. "That girl? She's a high-class whore that I
brought from São Paulo. But she's of no use to me, I'm
sending her back. Meanwhile she'll stay in the bathroom."

No, I couldn't count on Nunho. Or on any member of
Benjamim's family. Only on his friends.

We—the Captain, Orígenes, Elvira, and myself—held a
meeting. We came to a conclusion: it was essential that we
bring about a reconciliation between Samir and Benjamim.
We devised a plan. Under the pretext of celebrating something
or other, Orígenes would throw a party at the temple, to
which the two men would be invited, and when they met
face-to-face we would make them patch up their quarrel.

Elvira, whom Samir visited from time to time, would talk to
the Palestinian. I would take care of Benjamim.

Senhor Arão and Dona Frima agreed to our plan. And so
did Sula. It was heartbreaking, she told me, to see Benjamim,
unable to sleep, pace the bedroom back and forth all night long,
muttering threats against Samir.

Yes, it was high time this feud came to an end. Trying to
appear nonchalant, I spoke to Benjamim. He looked at me
with suspicion but ended up accepting the invitation.

The Captain and I were the first to arrive at the temple.
Samir came soon after, together with Peep-Less. But Benjamim
was late, which got me worried. Had he changed his mind?
All of us were already gathered around the table, laden with
assorted cakes and canapes, when Benjamim and Sula arrived.
As soon as he saw Samir, he wanted to beat a retreat, but Sula
and I held him back. Stop this nonsense, I said, it's so
childish, let's put an end to all this foolishness once and for all.

Somewhat reluctant, Benjamim let us take him to Samir, who,
frowning, pretended not to see him. We made them shake
hands. That's better, said Orígenes, and Elvira added: There's
no reason to quarrel, my dears, Rua Voluntários is big enough
to hold all of us, believe me, I know from experience. We
laughed; Benjamim and Samir were compelled to join in the
laughter. Seizing on the opportunity, Orígenes took a sheet of
paper from his pocket. It was the peace treaty that he had
written. Among other things it stipulated that Samir and
Benjamim were to abide by certain rules when accosting
shoppers on Rua Voluntários: Anyone walking from the bus
station toward the city center would fall to Samir; anyone
walking in the opposite direction would fall to Benjamim. Acts of
sabotage were forbidden; advertising would have to be
conducted within specified limits.

They hesitated, Benjamim and Samir did, but ended up
signing the paper—then suddenly they embraced and we
broke into applause. The Captain opened a bottle of wine under
the protests of Orígenes (wine here in the temple, that's a
sacrilege), and proposed a toast to peace.

The wine wasn't all that good, but we emptied the bottle.
Everybody was happy; Elvira suggested that we play Sula's
game—The Road to Jerusalem. Samir, who was telling a joke
to the Captain, was annoyed; but Benjamim was all fired up:
Come on, Samir, it's great fun.

We arranged the chairs in a circle, then smiling, we positioned
ourselves around them. Smiling and nervous. The Captain
took the harmonica from his pocket and began to play "A
Jardineira." Now! shouted Benjamim, and we broke into a
trot, and faster and faster we went. The music stopped, we
scrambled for the chairs, sat down—Sula was eliminated. In
the second round Elvira was eliminated, then Orígenes, then
Peep-Less. The Captain was now playing "A Carreirinha," a
lively gaucho tune. I was watching Benjamim. He looked as if
drugged, his eyes wide open, his mouth agape, his shirt
drenched in sweat. I was hoping I could beat Samir to the chair
in the next round, so that only Benjamim and I would
remain—the two friends; there would be no misunderstanding
between us. But I was out of luck. When the music stopped,
as I hesitated between the two remaining chairs, Benjamim and
Samir sat down, leaving me standing, somewhat bewildered. I
had been eliminated.

Benjamim and Samir, Samir and Benjamim. No longer running
but walking very slowly, they were circling the only remaining
chair, their eyes fixed on each other, but without hatred—or
rather, with hatred, but not just hatred, with fear and glee,
too. The two men, at once hunter and quarry, were relishing
that moment. The Captain, frightened, kept glancing at me as
if to ask for help. Stop! I shouted. The music stopped. Shoving
each other, the two men made a dash for the chair. For a few
seconds they grappled together, panting, until Samir finally
succeeded in sitting down. Then Benjamim collapsed and
rolled across the dusty floor.

We rushed to his aid. Get up, I said, pulling Benjamim by
the arm, don't lie there. I can't, he moaned, my leg hurts real
bad, I'm afraid it's broken. We'd better call an ambulance,
said Orígenes. Elvira went out to make the phone call. The

ambulance came. Two male nurses picked up Benjamim, laid
him on a stretcher, took him away. But just before the door
banged shut, I saw—and it made my blood freeze—the white
of an eye glowing in the semidarkness.

We went to the hospital and stood waiting in the hallway
while Benjamim was getting medical attention. It was taking a
long time, we were beginning to worry, when the doctor finally
appeared. Did he break his leg, doctor? asked Sula. Yes, he
replied. The hesitating: There's another problem. . . . Then
quickly amending himself: We can talk about it later.

An attendant was bringing Benjamim in a wheelchair, his leg
in a cast. We rushed up to him, Sula asking if he was all
right, Samir, distressed, apologizing. Everything's fine, Benjamim
kept saying, everything's fine.

I drew the doctor aside. What's wrong with him? I asked.
You can tell me, I'm a childhood friend, practically a brother.
The doctor looked at me; he was hesitating. It's a serious
matter, he finally said. He was choosing his words carefully: I
can't be sure yet, do you understand? I can't be one hundred
percent sure, but it's quite possible that he's got cancer, see?
Bone cancer, it's really serious.

Elvira was just then calling me to help Benjamim into a taxi.
Lifting him out of the wheelchair, I carried him out to the
street. Rather apathetic as he was, he let himself be carried
without making any fuss. He didn't weigh much—and at that
moment I was reminded of the Book of Daniel in the Bible:
You've been weighed on the scales and found wanting. And it
seemed to me that Benjamim, too, was found wanting; he was
so light, poor fellow.

I didn't return home. The Captain and I sat down on the
curb of the sidewalk in front of the bar. It was the Captain who
broke the silence: Funny, I've just now remembered that
today is the anniversary of my father's death, he said. It's been
twenty-two—no. Twenty-three years. A long time. Poor Father.
He drowned, poor fellow. He drowned because he was much
too proud.

He interrupted himself, remained silent for a few minutes, then continued.

"One winter at dawn we were inspecting the *Netuno*, our best ship, which was just back from shipyard where it had been for repairs. My father, who was standing at the bow, leaned out too far to look at something—and fell into the water. An old hand at sailing, and yet he fell into the water, my boy! He disappeared, and soon reappeared, snorting, furious. I couldn't help laughing, which only made him even more furious. I lowered a lifeboat; I wanted to pull him out of the water. But he refused my help. I don't need your help, he said, I can manage on my own. Twice he submerged in that dirty, ice-cold water, and twice his head rose to the surface, bobbing amid the rotten oranges floating about. You can help me now, if you want, he said, feigning indifference. I reached my hand out, he grabbed it, I tried to pull him out of the water, but couldn't. He was such a huge, fat man, and I didn't have enough strength. I said you could help me, he bellowed. I'm doing my best, I replied, trying to keep cool and collected, but I was already worried. Three or four bums loafing on the pier were laughing at us. Hurry up, said my father, what are you waiting for? I don't want to be a laughingstock to that riffraff over there. Again I grabbed him, and again he slipped away from me—he submerged, then rose to the surface. Help me, he yelled, I'm drowning. It was terrible to watch, Paulo. I tried again, I couldn't, he disappeared into the water, and I still remember the look in his eyes before he went down for the last time. It's hopeless, the eyes were saying. There was no accusation. Despair, yes, and resignation, perhaps even indignation, but no anger. No anger toward me. My father had forgiven me. I plunged myself into the water, brought him to the surface, and with the help of the bystanders, laid him on the boat. He was already dead. His watch was hanging from the chain fastened to his vest. It was working, and it still works."

The Captain sighed.

"By the way, do you realize what time it is?" He looked at his watch. "Three o'clock, Paulo. I must be going now."

*   *   *

I remained sitting there, staring at the street. What did I see? Paving stones damp with dew? The granular surface of the asphalt? Or potholes disclosing the paving stones underneath the asphalt? I no longer remember. That year was 1969, but I don't remember the year when Rua Voluntários was asphalted, nor the year when the streetcars were taken off the streets, nor the year when the Maipu closed down, nor the year when President Costa e Silva died. Neither do I remember what happened in the country in 1969: What was the minimum wage then? What was the exchange rate on the dollar? How much did a liter of gas cost? I didn't own a car then, and I still don't. And who was that cloaked man hurrying past me? A thief? An urban guerrilla? Doutor Alfredo? Poor Benjamim. And those Voluntários de Pátria, the Volunteers of the Fatherland, who were they? Yes, I know that they were involved in the war Brazil waged against Paraguay in the nineteenth century, but who were they? What did they look like? How old were they, what was their weight, their height? Where did they come from? What did they live on? If they lived on meat turnovers, what kind of filling did the meat turnovers have? How did they dress? What form of transportation did they use? Which were their favorite songs? What did they think of foreigners? Why, and in which direction, did they march? How well did they fight? Who did they fuck? Did they suffer from acne? What kind of slang did they use? What kind of timepiece told them the time? What books did the literate among them read? What did the peasants among them think of the agrarian reform? If they could, would they turn their firearms against their oppressors? What cigarette brands did they smoke? Whom did they love? How did they die? Did they die screaming? Did they open their eyes wide? Poor Benjamim. Did they die like flies? Like ants? History certainly wasn't my forte. Where are they buried? Do they rest in peace? Who remembers them? Poor, poor Benjamim.

It was growing light and the stores were beginning to open their doors when I got home. Maria Amélia, tearful, sat in the living room, waiting for me: You're shameless, Paulo. You

spend your nights with this Elvira, with this whore; what are
your children going to think of you?

I sat down beside her, embraced her, asked for her forgiveness.
Sullen at first, she kept pushing me away, she didn't want to
talk to me. Afterward she relented, and kissed me. I laid my
head in her lap, then, exhausted, I fell alseep.

In their restless sleep—if restless it was—of whom did they
dream? The Volunteers, I mean.

TWO WEEKS LATER BENJAMIN WAS HOSPITALIZED AT THE
Beneficência Portuguesa Hospital. Nunho, informed of his
brother's condition, came from São Paulo and said that he
would look after everything, that he would foot the bill. That
the family should do everything that was necessary. As it turned
out, there wasn't much that could be done; the tests confirmed
the initial diagnosis. It was cancer all right, terminal cancer. A
matter of months, said the doctor.

Nothing was disclosed to Benjamim. He had consented to
being hospitalized in order to have X rays taken. I've never
been ill, he said to me, worried. I can't stand these hospital
beds. During the first few days he kept nagging the doctors
to tell him what kind of illness he had: evasive, they would say
someting about rheumatism, uric acid. But if it's just
rheumatism, why can't I go home? he would protest, his eyes
fraught with anxiety. They would explain that his condition
required an initial course of treatment, blood serum, nutrients.
But Benjamim couldn't resign himself to the situation; he
wanted to go home, look after the store. One day he even got
out of bed and tried to put on his clothes: weak as he was,
and with his leg still in a cast, he fell down and had to call out
to Sula, who was in the bathroom. With great difficulty she

managed to lay him in bed, and then, unable to contain herself, she burst into tears. Benjamim kept looking at her, without understanding. But after that incident he stopped asking questions. And he no longer said anything about leaving the hospital.

Every day one of us—myself, or the Captain, or Orígenes, or Elvira, or Peep-Less, or Samir—would walk up Rua Coronel Vicente to visit him at the hospital. I was a more frequent visitor than the others: I would sit down by Benjamim's bed, and the two of us would talk. Avoiding the subject of his illness, I would hark back to our school days—the history classes, our attack on the Shadow's house. I would reminisce about the Maipu, and recall the freakish characters we used to know.

"Remember that guy we called Lick-Smooth? And what about the Turd-Grinder, hmm, Benjamim?"

Benjamim would smile as we recalled Lick-Smooth, a little old man whose hair shone with Gumex Brilliantine, and the Turd-Grinder, a huge fat man who was always sniffing and inspecting the soles of his shoes. I wonder if I'll ever see any of those people again, Benjamim would say, if I'll ever see Rua Voluntários again. That's bullshit, I would say. We'll still be playing the field for a long time, Benjamim. We'll still be dancing the buttock jig, there's still plenty of fooling around for us, you bet there is.

By then he already knew how seriously ill he was, but he put on a brave front, perhaps to cheer up his friends, his parents, his wife. Only once did he seem to lose courage. It was a Sunday afternoon, we were all gathered in his room, there was an animated conversation going on—if I'm not mistaken, we were discussing soccer, two major teams were playing on that day—when Benjamim said out of the blue:

"I don't want to die."

Confused, anguished, we stopped short. There was a silence. I don't want to die, he repeated. Elvira had to turn her face to the wall to hide her tears.

You know, he went on in a very feeble voice, I've never been to Jerusalem. Nowadays it's so easy to travel, what with all these tours, all these flights available, and yet I've never been to Jerusalem, I've never seen the Wall, I've never touched it.

And that's what I need, my friends: if only I could touch the Wall, the stones of the Wall, I think I would get better, perhaps even cured, who knows? Forgive me, Samir, I know you're Jordanian.

Then, gasping for breath, Benjamim fell silent. There was a tense silence, which Samir finally broke. I'm not Jordanian, Benjamim, he said in a low voice, I'm Palestinian.

Benjamim looked at him. "Jordanian. Palestinian—there are no such things, Samir."

"But that's what I am—Palestinian," persisted Samir. "And Jerusalem is my hometown."

Benjamim made no reply. He remained silent, staring at the ceiling. Suddenly, turning his face to Samir, Benjamim fixed his gaze on him, his eyes glittering. The Pool of Siloam! he cried out. Samir didn't understand. The Pool of what? he asked, puzzled. The Pool of Siloam, repeated Benjamim, and then spurred on a by a burst of energy: You heard me, man! The Pool of Siloam!

Samir's face lit up. "Why, yes, of course!" Then taking up the challenge: "All right, the Gihon Spring."

"Right on!" said Benjamim. After thinking for a moment, he launched another attack: "Dormition Abbey."

Samir: "The Church of the Holy Sepulcher."

Benjamim: "The Via Dolorosa."

Samir: "The Mount of Olives."

Benjamim: "Omar's Mosque."

Samir, laughing: "The Al-Aqsa Mosque, of course."

In silence we watched the scene, not knowing what to do, or what to say.

Benjamim: "The Church of the Ascension."

Samir: "The Basilica of the Holy Heart."

Benjamim: "The Convent of the Carmelites."

Samir: "The Paternoster Cloister."

Benjamim: "The Tomb of David is carved in ..."

Samir: "Rock. And what's inside?"

Benjamim: "A huge sarcophagus."

Gasping for breath, Benjamim fell silent. Sula, her eyes puffy, signaled to me: she wanted us to leave. But Benjamim was already launching another attack: "Jaffa Gate!"

Samir: "The New Gate!"

Benjamim, lifting himself up with difficulty: "Damascus Gate!"

Samir, vacillating: "Herod's Gate!"

Benjamim, feeling close to victory: "The Lion's Gate!"

Samir made no reply.

"The Lion's Gate," insisted Benjamim.

"I don't know," Samir admitted, and Benjamim, triumphant: "Zion's Gate! Zion's Gate!"

Benjamim broke down and cried convulsively while we sat watching, uncertain whether to stay or to leave.

When he calmed down, I rose to my feet. "We'd better go now, Benjamim."

"No," he said. "I don't want any of you to leave, not yet. . . . Stay a little longer. I don't want you guys to leave with a bad impression." He smiled. "Why don't we play the game, The Road to Jerusalem?"

"Here?" I asked, perplexed.

"Yes, here, why not? Put the chairs around the bed."

We moved the bed to the middle of the room, then put the chairs around it. Taking his harmonica from his pocket, the Captain began to play. The first one to be eliminated was Peep-Less, who fell to the floor as he and Elvira scrambled to get possession of a chair—which made Benjamim laugh a great deal. Then Sula was eliminated. Then Elvira, and finally, I defeated Samir, and was the only one left. We'd better go now, I said. You must get some rest, Benjamim.

It was a relief to find ourselves finally outside on the street. Oh, God, do I ever need a drink, said the Captain.

We came to the bar. I opened the door, we walked in, then I closed the door behind us. I poured each of us a glass of cognac. We sat drinking in silence. I'm a tough man, the Captain said finally, but I confess it was more than I could bear to see poor Benjamim, practically a corpse, shouting *Zion's Gate, Zion's Gate.* You were a hero, Elvira said to Samir. Well, poor fellow, he deserved it, Samir replied.

"What really impresses me," said Orígenes, "is this deep

devotion of his to Jerusalem. Imagine, a city he has never
even seen. You guys are unbelievers, you can't understand the
power of this feeling. Maybe Samir here understands what I'm
saying."

Samir said nothing; melancholy, he continued to munch on a
meat turnover. Everybody was silent again, a silence broken
only by Elvira's sobs.

As for me, what I was feeling wasn't just sadness. It was
anger, too, at my being so powerless, so unable to help a
dying friend.

One afternoon Sula came over to the bar to see me. She
unburdened herself: I can't take it any longer, Paulo, you
can't imagine what I've been going through.

Looking after Benjamim was becoming harder and harder.
Her parents-in-law weren't any help to her; on the contrary,
their jeremiads only upset her even more. As for Nunho,
well, he was paying for all the hospital expenses, all right, but
he never came; he would just phone from São Paulo once in a
while to inquire after his brother's health.

Poor Sula. She had lost weight; there were dark circles under
her eyes. It's been weeks since I last had a good night's sleep,
she complained. I offered to sit up with Benjamim that night.
She was reluctant at first—Dona Frima will say I'm an awful
daughter-in-law—but ended up accepting my offer.

What a night it was! When I arrived, Benjamim was already
in a state of agitation, moaning, at times screaming with
pain, and so he remained, notwithstanding the injections of
morphine the nurse was giving him almost every hour. He
kept tossing about, and I had to hold his arm down so that he
wouldn't yank out the intravenous tube.

About three o'clock in the morning he quieted down: I
thought he had fallen asleep. Gingerly I started to get ready
to lie down for a while.

"Paulo."

No, he wasn't asleep.

I got up, and drew near. "I'm here, Benjamim. Relax,
everything is all right."

He wasn't listening: his eyes were fixed on the ceiling; his profile, made even more grotesque by his extreme gauntness, was outlined against the faint light.

"It's terrible, Paulo."

"What's terrible, Benjamim?"

"This pain, Paulo. Unbearable. It's demoralizing. As if I weren't demoralized enough, Paulo. I'm so . . . ill. So weak. I wish I could die right now and get it over with, Paulo. I envy your mother. Honest, I do."

With my lips already trembling, I was trying to pull myself together.

"What nonsense, Benjamim."

"But it's true, Paulo. From you I don't have to hide anything do I? I'm fucked out, Paulo, I'm—"

He interrupted himself and let out a terrible howl. I rushed to him: Is there anything I can do for you, Benjamim? Tell me, what can I do for you? I was in such a cave of despair, I couldn't bear to see him like that, in that agitation.

"Get me out of here," he moaned, his eyes closed, his face contorted with pain. "Get me out of the hospital, Paulo. Take me to Jerusalem, Paulo. I want to die in Jerusalem. Please, Paulo!"

The nurse came rushing in, a syringe in her hand. We both held Benjamim down, and she gave him a shot in the buttock. He floundered in bed for a while and finally fell asleep. But I didn't sleep. I couldn't. Not after what I had seen.

That image kept haunting me—that image of a thin, hairy buttock covered with needle marks, and even bedsores. A buttock from a concentration camp.

To die in Jerusalem. Poor Benjamim. Wouldn't a man who was suffering so much, a condemned man, have the right to die in Jerusalem? I mustered enough courage to put the question to Sula. The two of us were in the corridor of the hospital, waiting for the doctor to finish examining Benjamim.

"To take Benjamim to Jerusalem? You're out of your mind, Paulo."

There was displeasure and censure in her voice. Even so, I persisted.

"Why not, Sula? It's the poor fellow's last wish."

Startled, she looked at me.

"Not that he's in critical condition," I hastened to amend myself. "But after all, if that's what he wants . . . if that's what he wants most . . ."

At a loss of words, I fell silent. Sula was no longer looking at me.

Then it occurred to me: "There might be a doctor there, a specialist that might be able to help him. After all, it's an advanced country, and who knows."

"Please, Paulo." She clutched my arm. "Let's not talk about it anymore, okay? Don't add to our woes. Please. You're a friend; there's no need for me to go into explanations. Please."

"All right. All right," I said.

But the idea kept nagging me. On the following day in the bar, I told the Captain, Orígenes, and Peep-Less everything that had happened, Benjamim's request, my talk to Sula. They were deeply touched. Well, I'll be damned, said the Captain, I'll be damned. Orígenes agreed with me; he thought it was quite possible that Benjamim would get better, if not cured, if he were to go to Jerusalem. He mentioned cases of people with gallstones whom the Reverend Jonathan had cured by placing *The Book of Revelations* on their bellies.

"True, cancer is far worse, it can't even be compared with gallstones. But it's also true that faith can move mountains. And if it can move mountains, then it can also cure cancer."

The Captain, too, agreed with me; and so did Elvira, who had just walked in. The only dissident was Peep-Less, resentful because we wouldn't give his smelly elixir to Benjamim.

"You guys look down your nose at a domestic product. You'd rather take the fellow to a foreign country. You'll regret it. It's going to be much more expensive and it won't do him any good."

At that point in time a strange incident involving Peep-Less and Elvira took place, an incident that was to have repercussions later. One evening Peep-Less approached Elvira: I want to spend the night with you.

None of us had ever seen Peep-Less with a woman. The
Captain suspected he was somewhat gay; even Elvira would
say that she had never seen a gaucho who looked so unmacho.
But I thought otherwise: Peep-Less was like that due to
homesickness and grief over the loss of his wife and children.
Whatever the reason, there was no question that Peep-Less
seemed to shun women. Elvira was surprised, but as she told us
later, in her profession you don't ask questions, and if the
client pays, everything is fine. The two of them reached an
agreement. On that same night Peep-Less knocked on Elvira's
door. He went in, carefully deposited the valise containing
Pascoal and Catarina and the small suitcase with the flasks of
elixir in a corner. Without a word, he took off his clothes,
folded them, laid them on a chair. Lying naked in bed, Elvira
waited. Peep-Less threw himself upon her and tried clumsily to
shove himself in. Take it easy, Elvira kept saying, trying hard
not to laugh.

Suddenly she let out a yell: Pascoal and Catarina had escaped
from the valise and the enormous snake was creeping along
the edge of the bed. Never mind! Shouted Peep-Less, don't get
distracted now that I'm almost coming. But it's a snake,
Elvira protested.

"It's tame! It's tame!"

Tame or not, Elvira wasn't going to take any chances.
Shoving Peep-Less aside, she jumped out of bed, grabbed a
shoe, and hit the snake in the head. The long spike heel
(a source of pleasure for her fetishist clients) penetrated the
skull, where it remained lodged. Catarina fell to the floor,
where it was shaken by convulsions until it lay still: dead. Ah,
you bitch, you've killed Catarina, yelled Peep-Less. And why
shouldn't I? said Elvira, her anger matching his. A snake in
my bed and you think I wouldn't kill it? It's unbelievable that
someone would bring such animals here.

Peep-Less was no longer listening; he was upset. Lifting the
snake from the floor, he yanked the shoe out of its skull, then
threw the shoe away (Hey, easy now, Elvira protested). He
rolled up the body of the ophidian, then put in the valise, to
which Pascoal, frightened by all the uproar, had already retreated.
He got dressed, picked up his belongings, and departed

without paying any attention to Elvira's hue and cry: And my
money, you shit heel? What about my money?

In spite of Sula's objections, I talked to Senhor Arão and
Dona Frima about our idea of taking Benjamim to Jerusalem.
Again I reasoned: It was the last wish of a dying man, it
might do him good, and so on and so forth. All to no avail.
Like their daughter-in-law, they thought it was a crazy plan.
Senhor Arão even took offense: How dare you come up with
such stupid ideas when Benjamim is dying; it's shameless,
Paulo, and I thought you were a friend.

But among the rest of us (us: the Captain, Elvira, Orígenes,
and myself; as for Samir and Peep-Less, the latter still badly
shaken by the death of Catarina—well, they never said
anything about this matter), the idea of taking Benjamim to
Jerusalem had taken root, and we wouldn't give it up because
of his family opposition. In a way we were his family, too; we
had rights and obligations. Besides, Benjamim himself had
requested that we take him to Jerusalem. Unless, the Captain
would reason, he said this while raving, delirious with pain.

I decided to put the matter to the test. Taking advantage of
Sula's brief absence from the room during one of my visits to
the hospital, I leaned over Benjamim and whispered: This thing
about Jerusalem, is it for real? He stared at me without
comprehending. He was so debilitated by the illness that he was
unable to latch on to a hint.

"Jerusalem," I persisted. "Jerusalem, Benjamim. Remember?
You were talking to me about it, buddy. We're planning to
take you to Jerusalem, Benjamim. The Captain, Orígenes, myself,
all of us."

A brief flash of light lit up his gaunt face. Go ahead with it,
he murmured in a feeble, hoarse voice. Your parents and your
wife are opposed, I said, but we intend to take you there
anyway. Go ahead with it, he repeated. We will! I said,
almost shouting, already excited. We sure will!

Easier said than done. Even getting Benjamim out of the

hospital would pose a major problem, but taking him to
Jerusalem seemed simply impossible, as we later realized while
discussing the matter. The airfare was terribly expensive, none
of us had that kind of money, not even enough money for a
down payment; besides, all of us wanted to accompany
Benjamim. I'm his best friend, I would say, to which Elvira
would retort: And what about me? After all, it was from me
that he learned how to screw, Paulo. Orígenes would mention
the spiritual affinities between them, whereas the Captain felt
that since Benjamim had put up with his stories for so many
years, he owed him a debt of gratitude. Samir and Peep-Less
were saying nothing, but we considered them likely candidates,
too—even though it wouldn't be easy for Samir to enter
Israel, of course, but it was obvious that he felt remorse over his
behavior toward Benjamim, even though we kept telling him
he was in no way to blame for the poor fellow's illness. As for
Peep-Less, he grew more and more uncommunicative. Recently
he had chummed up with Big Dog, and the two of them were
often seen together in the bars of the Public Market area,
talking in whispers. Are you in some kind of business with Big
Dog, Peep-Less? Orígenes would ask, chagrined because the
hawker had stopped frequenting the temple. It's none of your
damn business, Peep-Less would reply with a scowl on his
face. Whenever Orígenes asked him if he intended to accompany
Benjamim to Jerusalem, Peep-Less would say neither yes nor
no.

We had reached an impasse: too many candidates—not
enough money. At one time we even tried to exclude each
other mutually. You can't go, Elvira, Orígenes would say,
there's no way Big Dog is going to let you. To which she
would retort: And what about you and that Irmgard of yours;
you can't even take a step without asking for your wife's
permission. If I were you, the Captain would warn me, I
wouldn't leave the bar unattended, to which I would reply
gruffly that I didn't need his advice. Then I in turn would
reason with Samir that it was probably inadvisable for him to
return to the city he had left. With his Levantine features, he
would only arouse suspicion and possibly jeopardize the whole
project. To which Samir, incensed, would say: If Benjamim can

see Jerusalem, why can't I? It's my city, Paulo. I'm not from
Assyria, nor from Babylon, nor from Lebanon; I'm from
Jerusalem, my friends, and I want to revisit the city where I
was born, right? I want to see the Jordan River again, right?

Yes, sure, he was right, but even so, he would arouse
suspicion. As a matter of fact, my suspicions weren't about
Samir only. At one point I began to wonder if each one of us
didn't have ulterior motives, motives unrelated to our friendship
for Benjamim.

Elvira, for instance, probably looked on the journey to
Jerusalem as some kind of pilgrimage, a way to expiate her
sins, a way to present herself to that brother of hers who ran a
hostel for pilgrims as a devout Christian about to walk the
Via Dolorosa. The Captain probably hoped to see Captain
Andreas again, the man who had played such an important
role in his life; and Orígenes—well, the Reverend Jonathan's
Book of Revelations could well be sufficient reason for him to
set out on this journey, not to mention Irmgard, who was
enough to make any man want to run away. As for Peep-
Less, well, I had no idea, for he never said anything—and I
must admit that I never really counted on him. And as for
Samir—who was this Samir anyway? Was he really from
Jerusalem? Did he have relatives there? Did he really like my
meat turnovers as he kept proclaiming to all and sundry? In
what language did he speak to his brother? And what did
they talk about? What kind of food did they eat when the two
of them had a meal at the back of their store? There was
something fishy about that man. Couldn't he be a terrorist who
was returning to Jersualem on the pretext of accompanying a
sick man, there to commit sabotage?

Yes, somewhere along the line I began to entertain suspicions.
Even about myself. What impelled me to set out on this
journey? Kindness or boredom? I was then going through a
difficult phase in my life. Here in the bar I would look at the
meat turnovers and ask myself: So, is this it? Is this it then, to
my dying day? The bar, Rua Voluntários, and Porto Alegre?
By that time many of my old school chums had moved to the
center of the country—and even to other countries. Some were
now business executives, others had joined the Civil Service, still

others had received scholarships to study abroad. Aninha was a fashion model; sometimes I saw her on television. And what about me? Would I stay on in Porto Alegre? At home I would watch Maria Amélia furtively: love or habit? She had changed; she was no longer the teenager with whom I had fallen in love at first sight. She had changed, and so had I. As for the children—yes, they were my sons, I loved them, but when they pestered me to get them this or that, it was sheer hell.

To go on a jaunt at that point in time would be just what the doctor ordered. Moreover, once the airplane reached a certain altitude (say, ten thousand meters) and passed a certain point (the meridian of Greenwich, or the legendary island of Cyprus) I would perhaps feel suddenly liberated, like a rocket escaping from the Earth's pull of gravity. At that altitude, at that longitude, suspended in time between the sky (God? No, I wasn't worried about Him) and the sea, I would be able to have a different, more encompassing view of the world as I floated amid the clouds in the immense, salutary silence so necessary after the daily din of Rua Voluntários, with its hawkers crying their plastic combs, their Argentinian apples, their miraculous herbs, with the infernal noises of cars honking, radios blaring. I yearned for silence so that I could think, find myself. The sky above, the sea below, the past behind, slowly dissolving like the smoke of the jet engines, and an uncertain future ahead; and to my left, Benjamim, his weight down to fifty kilograms, poor fellow, would be sitting or even lying on a stetcher (we knew very little then, as we later found out, about regulations governing the transport of sick people on international flights). And finally, to my right, a beautiful, elegant, mysterious passenger, perhaps French, or perhaps Swedish or Uruguayan, or even Brazilian, as long as she lived in an aristocratic neighborhood of Rio or São Paulo (but she was definitely not from Porto Alegre, for it was from Porto Alegre that I was trying to escape). I would strike up a conversation with this young lady, we would become friends, and after the martinis we would exchange confidences. She—a journalist, or a writer, or an embassy secretary, or an exotic millionaire—would be flying to Jerusalem on business or perhaps to find meaning in her life (recently divorced, etc.). We would agree to see each other again. On that day, after leaving Benjamim near that Wall of his, the stranger and I, holding hands, would stroll about the picturesque alleys of the Old City. We would go sight-seeing (Dormition Abbey, the Lion's Gate, the Al-Aqsa Mosque); after some haggling in the Arab and Jewish markets, we would buy souvenirs, then late in the afternoon, we would stop somewhere for a cup of coffee. After taking Benjamim back to the hotel, we would go out for dinner, then go dancing at a sophisticated nightclub. Afterward we would make love on the hills of Jerusalem—who knows, maybe under the branches of a centuries-old olive tree. At that moment I would be free from the Lusitania Bar, free from Rua Voluntários, free from everything. When Benjamim got better— and how could he not get better there in Jerusalem?—I would send him back home and I would live in Europe, perhaps in Paris, in the apartment that my lady friend certainly owned in the Champs-Elysées; and I would own a Maserati and spend the summers in Cannes.

Everybody else felt just as excited. We got carried away by our ecstatic visions, visions akin to those of my ancestor Sisenando, the Mute, who had crossed the lands of Europe and the Mediterranean Sea in search of the Holy Grail. But we weren't a merry and bloodthirsty bunch like his group had been. Well, merry yes, even more than merry—jubilant—but not bloodthirsty. We had no intention of killing anyone; it was life that we were after. All we wanted was to arrive in Jerusalem, take Benjamim to the places he had been yearning to see—the Wall, among others—and soon return with our sick friend, we hoped, much better.

(And if he died? We never raised this possibility, but if he died—well, then he would die in Jerusalem, according to his wish.)

While we were having these discussions, elsewhere, on Rua da Praia, major business deals were being closed, great sums of

money kept changing hands. The stock market was buoyant.
People were buying and selling shares, pocket calculators were
quickly determining how much profit had been reaped.
Widows were selling their condominiums, others were pawning
the family jewelry. Foreign emissaries kept arriving in the
country to study the investment situation, the newspapers were
full of euphoric statements, computer monitors gyrated in a
frenzy. I'm sick and tired of this hand-to-mouth existence,
Maria Amélia kept saying. Munching on a meat turnover, my
mind on the journey, I would say nothing.

It's going to be all right, Benjamim, I would say every time
I visited him at the hospital. Sula thought I was referring to his
illness, when in fact I was talking about a journey, a long
journey to the Golden City. I was talking about Jersusalem.

Beautiful plans, beautiful dreams, secret motives perhaps—
but the fact is that we argued a lot here in the bar without ever
hitting upon a solution. The dificulties seemed to grow
greater and greater. We had no money; besides, it was unlikely
that we would be able to travel by air; the airline companies
would demand special precautions before allowing aboard someone
as seriously ill as Benjamim.
On a Saturday afternoon, after many bottles of beer, we came
to the realization that it would be impossible for us to carry out
our plan. And then we were in a slough of despondency. But
suddenly the Captain had a brainstorm.
"Hell, that's it!" he shouted, pounding the table with his fist.
"We'll go by boat, why not?"
Perplexed, we looked at one another. "By boat?" asked
Orígenes. "Whose boat, Captain?"
"Mine," he said. "My tugboat."
The tugboat—we had long forgotten that the Captain owned
a tubgboat, for he never talked about it. But on a tugboat?
To cross the ocean on a tugboat? Lunacy. Not at all, stated the
captain. You guys haven't seen my tugboat yet. A valiant boat

that has crossed the ocean several times. It's safer than any
transatlantic ocean liner.

"Don't you guys believe me?" He rose. "Come, let's go to the
pier."

We went to the pier and there was the tugboat.

It was old, possibly the oldest tugboat in the harbor. A big
but ramshackle tugboat, it looked as if it would fall apart in
the first windstorm. It needs some minor repairs, admitted the
Captain, and a nice coat of paint, but the hull is sound, the
engine is extremely powerful, not to say economical, and there's
room for all of us.

He showed us into some kind of a cubicle with berths: the
cabin.

"It's small, but we can all squeeze in. What we need is
transportation, not comfortable surroundings."

I want to make myself quite clear, said Elvira, nobody is
going to sleep with me. I'm going to spend the entire journey
praying; there won't be any hanky-panky. We laughed, but it
was a rather forced laugh. And what about the crew? Samir
wanted to know. Where is it going to stay? The Captain stared
at him, stunned: The crew, Samir? We are the crew, on this
boat there's room for nobody else but us. Besides, we want to
keep this journey wrapped in secrecy, don't we? We ourselves
will have to do all the work on board. But, protested Orígenes,
I've never been aboard a boat before, I know zilch about the
subject. Leave it to me, said the Captain. There's no mystery
about it, I'll teach you guys, it won't take you more than a
minute to learn.

"What's important is to have a good skipper, and all modesty
aside, you've got one in me."

Later, here in the bar, when the Captain and I were alone, I
asked him to talk in earnest. What did he think of this
voyage, wasn't it sheer madness? It is madness, he agreed, but
that's no reason to give it up.

Lighting the cigarette he had just rolled up, he took a long
drag.

"I come from a family of navigators, Paulo. From people that
won renown. I'm a descendant of the founders of the Hanseatic
League. There's no need for me to tell you about the Hanseatic

League; you must have learned about it in school. My
grandfather, my father, and my uncles used to crisscross the
rivers and lakes of this state of Rio Grande do Sul at a time
when accurate maps weren't even available. They would sail the
rivers up to their headwaters; they would load their boats
with oranges from the town of Taquari, with coal from the
town of São Jerônimo, with leather from the region of the
Vale dos Sinos. Always sailing back and forth—back and forth
they traveled, nothing stopped them sailing. They often set
out in bad weather and sailed in the worst possible storms. And
they always took me with them: I was a baby and already
sailing.... Brave people they were. They became famous;
there's even a street in Porto Alegre named after my grandfather.
True, a street in the suburbs, but even so ... When I die, not
even a blind alley will bear my name. And I don't even have
any offspring to give my name to. I have nothing. Do you
know why, Paulo?"

He drained his glass of beer.

"Because I was smart, Paulo. Smart and prudent. I thought
that the heyday of navigation was over, that it was time for
me to get out of the business. I sold the boats that I had
inherited to a major company. I made quite a bundle in the
transaction; it was a clever move. Give me another beer, will
you?"

I opened another bottle; he filled both our glasses.

"Except that I lost everything. In business deals, you know.
In investments. Disastrous investments. I was practically flat
broke. Then I decided to turn to navigation again. With what
little money I had left, I bought a tugboat. But the fact is that
by then the desire was no longer there. I stopped sailing, I
rented out the tugboat, that's how I earned a livelihood.
Imagine what my grandfather would say if he knew. Cheers,
Paulo!"

We drank to our health.

"So you see, this voyage is important to me. It's a voyage of
rehabilitation, know what I mean? Even if it's lunacy. Yep,
that's what it is."

Then rising to his feet: "That's what it is. I'm going home
now, Paulo."

(He lived in the Majestic Hotel. He liked that hotel because
the skywalks that linked it to the other old buildings reminded
him of a ship's gangway. From his bedroom—furnished like a
ship's stateroom, there were even scuttles on the wall, as well
as compasses, sextants, nautical charts—the Captain could see
the Guaiba River, the freighters with exotic names lying at
anchor in the harbor.)

We grew more and more excited about the project. Each
one of us had already devised an excuse to justify a thirty- or
forty-day absence—the anticipated duration of our voyage.
    Elvira had cooked up a story about having to visit her family
in the interior; she would play upon Big Dog's heart strings
by saying that her mother was seriously ill: He's got a mother,
too, so he knows what this means. Big Dog is not the bandit
you guys think he is; he's got feelings, too. Orígenes was going
to show Irmgard a letter inviting him to establish a temple of
the Lord's Companions in Cascavel, a small town in the state of
Paraná, a letter that would also mention a substantial amount
of money as payment for his services. Irmgard is crazy about
money, I think she'll let me go, he would say, wistful.
    Samir's pretext was a trip to São Paulo to purchase merchandise.
As for me, I was going to talk to Maria Amélia about the
possibility of opening a *churrascaria* in Rio, a restaurant specializing
in barbecued meat, Rio Grande do Sul style; she wouldn't have
to fry meat turnovers anymore, she would be able to devote
herself to opera singing, and, like her sister Lina, whom she
envied, she would be living in the heart of the country.
Peep-Less—well, Peep-Less continued to be uncommunicative, but
as far as I knew, leaving the city wouldn't pose a problem for
him. And as for the Captain—he owed no explanations to
anyone.
    We paid a stiff price for our passports. All of them false, of
course, the work of a former cop, one of Elvira's clients. They
didn't look too authentic, but if we happened to hit a snag in
Haifa, we would steer away from the harbor and come ashore
on that deserted beach where Andreas had delivered the
weapons: I think I remember where it is, the Captain would

say, which wasn't very reassuring, but that wasn't the worst of our uncertainties. We didn't even know if we would ever reach our destination.

We needed a name for our boat. *Captain Andreas* was the Captain's suggestion, Samir wanted an Arabic name, I forget what it was, and Orígenes kept alluding to *The Lord's Companions* or *The Reverend Jonathan*. Elvira wanted to call it either *Big Dog* or *Via Sacra*. We argued here in the bar for hours on end: after many a bottle of beer, my suggestion met with general approval: *Os Voluntários*, the Volunteers. It was our street and it was us, too. We drank a toast to the success of our expedition.

ONCE THE NAME HAD BEEN PAINTED ON THE BOW, WE WERE finally ready to set sail. And about time, too: Benjamim was much worse, growing weaker by the day. Rarely lucid, he went through periods of delirium, of agitation. So it was high time we set sail.

We would have to spirit Benjamim out of the hospital and take him to the boat: a quick, silent commando operation to be carried out in the dead hours of the night.

I remember that night very well. It happened back in December of 1970—we were going to celebrate Christmas on board, after we set off on our voyage. Although it's been a long time, I still remember that night very clearly. How could I ever forget it? Yeah, I do remember it.

A strange night. It wasn't cold, but around nine o'clock in the evening, the river became shrouded in mist, something unusual for that time of the year, but I regarded this fact as a good omen. The fog would hide our boat; nobody would notice our departure.

At ten o'clock I locked up the bar. Then I signaled to Samir, whose store was open late for the Christmas shopping. Orígenes was supposed to go from the temple straight to the pier, where Elvira would be waiting. At her request we had decided we wouldn't go as a group in order to avoid attracting attention. At 11:40, from the Majestic Hotel, the Captain phoned the reception desk at the Beneficiência Portuguesa Hospital, asking for Sula.

"It's urgent! A matter of life and death!"

As she went downstairs to answer the phone, we sneaked into the hospital—Samir and I disguised as nurses, and Elvira dressed in the nun habit she had acquired to satisfy one of her clients, who was unable to have sex with a woman unless she was dressed like a Carmelite nun. Meanwhile Orígenes and Peep-Less were waiting outside in Samir's big car, an old Cadillac.

Quickly we mounted the old wooden stairway and hurried down the dark corridors (and as we did so, I couldn't help thinking of the sanatorium where my mother had died). We entered Benjamim's room, which was faintly lit by a bedside lamp.

He raised his head slightly. "Who's there? Ah, you accursed creature! I'm not dead yet. Begone! Leave me alone!"

To whom was he speaking? To the Angel of Death? To King Solomon? To the Shadow? To Samir? To the King of the Rats? To Nunho? To his father? To his cancer? To a customer? Or was it just to Paulo, his childhood friend? Was it possible that Benjamim's now blurred (or now sharpened?) eyesight, and his final delirium (or final lucidity?) could detect wickedness beneath his friend's compassion and dedication?

There was no time to find out. It's us, your friends, Benjamim, I said, trying to calm him down. We came to rescue you.

With the utmost care—there were tubes attached to his veins—Samir and I laid him on a stretcher, and we went out. In the corridor we saw a figure. It was Sula returning to the sickroom; it looked as if the Captain hadn't succeeded in keeping her on the phone. Quick, through the back exit! Samir whispered.

We ran with the stretcher toward the stairway at the back.

"Wait!" Sula cried out. "Who are you carrying there?"

We tore down the stairs. Elvira dropped the drip bottle, which shattered with a loud noise. Stop, Benjamim kept moaning. For God's sake, stop, let me die here. But we couldn't stop, not now that we had set things in motion. We had to go ahead with the whole thing.

But Benjamim grabbed my hand. "It's no use, Paulo. It's beyond our reach. I mean, Jerusalem ... it's beyond our reach, Paulo. Please, just leave me here. Don't play this kind of trick on poor Sula."

We could hear her footsteps on the stairs; she was limping down the stairs.

"Benjamim! Where are you, Benjamim!"

"Here!" he cried out in a feeble, hoarse voice. "Here, Sula! Here! Come to me, Sula!"

"I can't, Benjamim. I've sprained my ankle. I can't walk, Benjamim."

Elvira grabbed me. Let's leave Benjamim here, please, Paulo. I pushed her away. Benjamim, frightened, was staring at me. Leave me here, Paulo, he beseeched. Leave me here.

I bent forward. "No, Benjamim. You will go now. It's too late to change your mind."

The tone of my voice startled even myself. It wasn't me speaking, it was Sisenando, the Mute—with the terrifying voice that Saracens had silenced by cutting off his tongue. *Now you will go.* There was nothing that Benjamim could say. He kept staring at me, his eyes wide open.

"Help!" It was Sula's voice. "Nurse! Help! They're taking Benjamim away!"

"She'll have the whole hospital after us," I said to Samir. "Let's get the hell out of here."

We left through the back entrance, then made a dash for the car. After placing the stretcher on the back seat, we got in the car.

"To the pier! Quick!"

Orígenes started the car, and off we went, at high speed. I turned to the backseat. Benjamim was quiet, not quite sitting up, rather sprawling out on the seat, with his eyes closed. Sighing, I mopped my forehead. Where's Peep-Less? I asked Orígenes.

"I don't know. He said he had something to do before the journey. He disappeared."

"The hell with him," I muttered. "We don't need him."

We were approaching the wharf, luckily deserted at that hour. Orígenes turned off the headlights; we got out of the car. Then we took Benjamim out, put him on the stretcher, and went to the tugboat.

The Captain, who had been waiting, helped us carry Benjamim. Is he all right? he asked. Yes, I said, looking at Benjamim, who remained motionless, his breathing stertorous, I think so. Nervous, we fumbled with the stretcher, but managed to carry him aboard. The boat engine was idling, which made the old, ramschackle boat vibrate. We succeeded in lying Benjamim on one of the berths. Is there anything you want, Benjamim? Elvira kept asking. Tea? Soup? But he made no reply. He remained quiet, motionless.

Where's Peep-Less? asked the Captain. I don't know, I replied. We'll have to sail without him, we can't wait. We changed our clothes. We were sweating profusely. Elvira was whispering a prayer. Finally each of us was at his post: the Captain at the helm, Samir and I on the upper deck. Orígenes was in charge of the engine room. He was knowledgeable about engines—as a traveling salesman he had often been forced to fix his car himself. Besides, the captain had given him a few lessons on how to operate the boat engine.

"Attention, men!" shouted the Captain. His face glowed; I had never seen him so happy. "Attention, crew of the *Voluntários*! Ready?"

We were ready.

"Weigh anchor! Cast off!"

Samir and I cast off moorings.

"I'm giving the helm a half turn to port," shouted the Captain. "Attention, engine room!"

"Ready!" shouted Orígenes from below.

"Easy! Forward!"

The engine began to rotate faster; the whole boat creaked and snapped as if it were about to disintegrate. Slowly we began to leave the wharf behind. Samir hollered: "Hey, guys! We are on our way! We sure are!"

The Captain, standing in the wheelhouse, his face lit up from below by a small lamp, which gave him a phantasmagorical appearance, continued to issue commands. "Helm at zero! Attention, machinist! Forward, at full speed!"

We were already about two hundred meters from the wharf.
It was the beginning of our voyage.

Out of the fog came a shout.

"Stop, you motherfuckers!" The voice sounded familiar: Big
Dog? Once again the shout echoed in the still of the night:

"Stop! I've told you to stop!"

It *was* Big Dog. A moment later he came into sight; standing
at the bow of a motorboat, he was aiming the powerful beam
of a searchlight at the *Voluntários*.

"You there in the motorboat! Get out of the way!" yelled the
Captain, irritated. Then recognizing the man: "But it's Big
Dog! What the hell are you doing there, Big Dog? You're
blocking our way, come on, get moving!"

"Like fucking hell I will!" Big Dog was in a rage. "What's
this idea of stealing a man's woman, Captain? Hand over
Elvira!"

On hearing the commotion, Elvira, who had been in the cabin
with Benjamim, came running to the gunwale, furious.

"I don't want to go back to you, Big Dog. I'm staying here
with my friends. I've had it with being bossed about, with
being exploited. From now on I'll be my own mistress!"

"Cut the crap!" hollered Big Dog. "Come right back. What's
Doutor Alfredo going to say?"

"Haven't you heard what he said, Elvira? Come back!"

That voice was very familiar. Shortly afterward Peep-Less
appeared beside Big Dog, magnificently attired in full gaucho
garb: hat with chin straps, white kerchief around his neck,
poncho, *bombachas*, boots, and spurs. A lasso in his hand. Are
you out of your mind, Santino? I shouted, calling him by his
real name so as to jolt him back into reality. It's us, man!
Your friends!

He ignored me. In a calm but surprisingly arrogant tone, he
warned: "I'm telling you Elvira, for the last time. Come
back."

"Shut up, you capon," said Elvira, taunting him. Peep-Less
made no reply. He unfolded the lasso, gyrated it over his
head, then cast it. The motorboat was some distance away—
about thirty meters—but it was a perfect shot.

"I did it, I did it, Big Dog," Peep-Less kept shouting. "I've lassoed Elvira!"

Infuriated, Elvira was trying to wriggle herself free. Big Dog and Peep-Less kept tugging at the lasso; I did my best to hold Elvira back. Samir acted promptly. Grabbing the knife the Captain was proferring, he cut the rope.

"Fuck you!" bellowed Big Dog, chucking away what remained of the lasso and pulling a gun. He aimed it at Samir—but at that moment the Captain commanded that the tugboat advance at full throttle against the motorboat. Big Dog was shooting at us nonstop, Elvira was screaming, I ducked to the floor, pulling her down with me, the two boats collided violently, there was a terrible blast in the engine room. The tugboat heeled over and began to sink. I crawled up to the wheelhouse. The Captain was slumped over the helm, his head literally shattered by a bullet. Beside him, Samir lay in a heap on the floor, with blood spurting out from a wound in his neck—he was dead. From the engine room, where a fire was blazing, dense, black smoke was rolling out. Orígenes! I yelled. There was no answer.

Rising to my feet, I grabbed Elvira, who was staring at me with glazed eyes, pushed her over into the water, then jumped after her. Just in the nick of time: the *Voluntários* sank quickly.

I emerged amid the debris. There was no sign of the motorboat. By my side, Elvira, half-drowned, was floundering. I somehow managed to take her to the wharf. I lifted her onto the stone steps, then I plunged into the water and returned to the spot where the *Voluntários* had sunk. I swam about, hoping to find Benjamim and Orígenes. I knew it was a hopeless search. It would have been impossible for Orígenes to have escaped from that fire blazing in the engine room; as for Benjamim . . . nothing could be done. Nothing, absolutely nothing could be done.

I swam back to the wharf: exhausted, gasping for breath, I sat down next to Elvira. At that moment the sirens began to wail—firefighters, policemen, ambulances speeding toward the scene. We rose to our feet and ran all the way to Elvira's room, where we took refuge. Taking off our clothes, which were dripping wet, we lay down. Elvira was trembling. What a calamity, Paulo, she said over and over again in a low voice. What a calamity.

I hugged her. As we stood in front of each other, I kept looking intently on her face, like an explorer scrutinizing a map. Like an explorer scrutinizing a map—with love. For it was love that I was feeling for Elvira at that moment. Not the unbridled passion that Paulo, the teenager, had once mistaken for love. But a more tranquil, more resigned feeling. Yes, it was with love that I was gazing at Elvira's face.

What I saw, now that the makeup was almost completely washed off by the water of the river, was a ravaged face, a mottled complexion, a fine web of lines under the eyes. I was following those tiny lines just as the Captain's ancestors must have followeed the rivers and their tributaries. I kept kissing that skin. And I kept kissing her faded lips and her breasts, already beginning to sag, and her belly, somewhat flabby, and her thick thighs and her legs with varicose veins. My love, I kept murmuring softly; saying nothing, she just kept staring at me. Who had ever spoken to her like this? Myself, perhaps, in former days; Benjamim, for sure. And nobody else.

We made love. Afterward, we lay side by side, staring at the ceiling. I fell asleep.

I slept the whole day. When I woke up, night was falling, Elvira, dressed, was packing a suitcase. I'm leaving, she said. Where are you going? I asked. Home, she said. Back to the farm, to my parents.

She sat down on the bed by my side, stroked my hair, kissed me. I was crying. I'm not ashamed to say that I was crying. I made no attempt to hold her back. She stood, picked up the suitcase, and left.

On the following day the police recovered the bodies of Samir and the Captain from the river. The newspapers had banner headlines: MASSACRE ON THE GUAIBA, read one such headline; RIVER SHOOT-OUT, said another. There were full-page stories with many photographs.

One of the news stories talked about a war between rival

gangs of drug traffickers. But we were not a gang, we were a group of friends, we wanted to help a sick buddy; that's what I told the chief of police when I was arrested for questioning. Nobody believed me. The situation became even worse when Doutor Alfredo stuck his nose into this matter. Thanks to his contacts, he had easy access to the case. And he was personally following the entire investigation.

On several occasions I saw Doutor Alfredo, always in a huff, arguing with the chief of police. Maybe Doutor Alfredo resented the fact that Elvira had ditched him; maybe he was afraid she might tattle on him—but of course, that's not what he talked about. He kept saying that he had been probing into subversive activities in Porto Alegre and that there was a connection between them and the projected voyage on the *Voluntários*. As evidence, he had in his possession an extremely valuable document—a black notebook carefully wrapped in plastic— found, according to him, in Orígenes's pocket: a diary. Until then I didn't even know of the existence of this diary, which apparently Orígenes stared keeping soon after he joined the Lord's Companions. When the notebook was shown to me, I pictured Orígenes writing in the cold, empty temple, with the rats galloping about—like Cheyennes besieging a fort—and Irmgard yelling at him from the back of the temple, calling him a good-for-nothing bum. I felt that in those pages Orígenes must have poured out his innermost feelings, hopes, and visions. There he talked about angels and demons, about King Solomon and the holy whale, about celestial squirrels and Jehovah. And he talked about Jerusalem. But Doutor Alfredo, who had read and reread the diary, thought otherwise. He interpreted what was written in those pages as a typical subversive plan. According to him, everything had started with the arrival in the country of an agent—possibly a double agent, for the man was American—whose code name (Doutor Alfredo relished the expression *code name*) was Reverend Jonathan. After setting up a cell called the Lord's Companions, its followers devised a daring plan: the occupation of one of the islands on the Guaiba River, where they would establish their headquarters. A veritable Cuba, just across from Porto Alegre.

The unraveling of this plot had been an arduous task even for an old hand like Doutour Alfredo. According to him, Orígenes's text had been hard to interpret because of the many code names. *Jerusalem*: a code name for island. *Wailing Wall*: the main stronghold. *Whale*: the submarine of the American agent. *The Book of Revelations*: Mao's book?

Doutor Alfredo would point to other clues; for example, the name of the boat.

"*Voluntários*, Volunteers. The Chinese who fought in Korea were called volunteers."

The explosion: loads of ammunition in the hold of the boat. "And what about the shoot-out?" the chief of police would ask.

"A war between factions. A commonplace among subversives. Trotskyites against Stalinists. The Chinese party line against the Russian party line."

The chief of police seemed unconvinced, but Doutor Alfredo would persist: I'm knowledgeable about this matter, Chief. I've done a lot of reading on the subject; I even have a specialized library. Besides, I've been conducting my own investigations. I walk about in disguise, eavesdropping on conversations that take place on street corners. That's how I've dragged many a commie out of the closet.

Then lowering his voice: "I even prowl Rua Voluntários. If you only knew, Chief . . ."

The police investigation dragged on; I was under arrest for several days. But I wasn't held incommunicado. Maria Amélia would visit me and break into tears: Just look at you, Paulo, a businessman thrown in jail like a criminal. People are even saying you're involved in drugs. You've put your family to shame; it's that woman, she turned your head. That Elvira, I hope she'll burn in hell.

Trying my best to comfort her, I said that everything would turn out all right, that I'd soon be home. In fact, however, I considered my situation pretty grim.

Surprisingly the Shadow didn't try to lay the whole mess at my door. On the contrary, he tried to help me. He called on his friend Doutor Alfredo. I don't entirely approve of my son-in-law, the Shadow said, but I can trust him. Doutor

Alfredo didn't want to hear about it: We can't put our trust even in a son, far less on a son-in-law; nobody is immune to the germ of subversion, my dear fellow. The Shadow then severed relations with Doutor Alfredo. And when things became even more complicated—the chief of police was now considering handing me over to the federal department of national security—there was a sudden turnabout. The owner of the motorboat that Big Dog had rented, angry at Big Dog's refusal to pay for the damages, came to the police station and blew the whistle on him. The man disclosed the hideout of Big Dog and Peep-Less—both of whom I had assumed to be dead.

They were arrested. The chief of police saw right away that they didn't look like Trotskyites, or Stalinists, or Maoists. He interrogated them, they told the whole story, and this time the chief of police believed what he heard.

It was only then that the bodies of Orígenes, which had been badly burned, and of Benjamim were recovered. The currents had carried them a long way.

Then the chief of police set me free so that I could go to Benjamim's funeral.

When I arrived at the cemetery, the burial ceremony was almost finished. I stood watching from a distance.

A handful of people: the family (except for Nunho, whose whereabouts nobody knew), a few acquaintances from Rua Voluntários, from Bom Fim. The soft weeping of Sula, the wailing of Dona Frima, the sighing of Senhor Arão, the chanting of the officiant mingled with the shrill chirping of the cicadas and the rustling of the wind in the trees. The coffin was lowered, shovelfuls of earth thudded upon it—and it was all over.

I didn't know what to do, whether to leave or talk to the family. They ignored my presence, but it was understandable that they should hate me, that they should blame me for Benjamim's death.

Even so, Senhor Arão came up to me. I know you did this for Benjamim, he said. You're a good friend, Paulo, it's all right.

I hugged him. Accept my condolences, I wanted to say, but through a slip of the tongue what came out was "have a pleasant journey." He didn't hear me, though; Dona Frima was already pulling him away. They left.

When I returned home, Maria Amélia and the children greeted me with shouts of joy. We celebrated with a sumptuous lunch and a lot of wine. Afterward, in my bedroom, I spent a long time cleaning the mud off my shoes with a spatula. While doing so, I kept thinking of Benjamim: the miniature Jerusalem, his bout of gonorrhea, the history classes, the musical chairs. *Here!* His cry, faraway, still reverberated in my ears.

I finished scraping the mud off the soles of my shoes. I examined them. They were clean. But only seemingly so, I knew. I knew that tiny, invisible particles of mud remained encrusted in the very texture of the leather. Only by discarding the shoes—something I would never do—would I get rid of those particles of mud. These are very good shoes, Benjamim had said to me in his store, when he sold me the pair at cost price. True: old shoes but very good. Sturdy.

I collected the detritus on a sheet of newspaper. Such precious things amid the clods of red, dense earth: crystals, tiny faceted stones. And a big black ant. An ant from the cemetery. Stirring, still alive. I thought I would leave it somewhere on the floor. But the thought of the ant about the house, hidden in cracks, growing old, the thought of the ant reappearing one day on my pillow or on my plate, bearing death, which was part and parcel of its tissues, bearing the image of Benjamim—was intolerable. Coming to this conclusion, I folded up the sheet of newspaper with the ant inside, then squashed it. The ant died, I think it did. But then it wasn't the only death in this story, was it? That's right.

So here I am, at the counter of the Bar-Restaurante, Lusitania, a fat, bald, mustachioed man selling meat turnovers to his patrons. I while away the time by telling stories and selling the meat turnovers that Maria Amélia prepares as she sings softly, sighing at times.

The bar continues to be our source of income. It yields only a small profit, we can't afford certain luxuries; traveling, for example, is out of the question. I'll never go to Jerusalem, where Sula went after Benjamim died.

The road to Jerusalem is much too long for me.

Sula, Irmgard—I wonder how they're doing. I've never heard from them again. I can imagine Sula living in a very old house, a thousand or more years old. I can imagine her leading a modest life, eating frugal meals—but in an atmosphere replete with intense existential experiences, mystical trance, ecstasy, fervor; I can picture her interrupting her reading of the Bible for a moment, and heaving a sigh of rapture over a passage in the Song of Songs that she has just finished reading. I can see her running to the Wall, there to invoke the soul of Benjamim, and it is possible that his soul is indeed there, fluttering amid the birds that at sunset gather on the Wall. The soul of Benjamim and the soul of Samir, why not?

147

As for Irmgard, I think she must be back in Bariloche; I picture her running barefoot in the birch groves, followed by her squirrels, gentle little animals with fluffy tails and lively eyes, one of which answers to the name of Orígenes.

I know that Senhor Arão and Dona Frima now live in São Paulo with Nunho, who, according to what Senhor Arão told me in a letter, is a different man—a reformed man, who is now in the construction business, rolling in money. At an enterpreneurs' convention he met my sister-in-law Lina. After discussing the money markets at length, they had dinner together, and a month later they were married. Dona Frima wasn't too pleased to see her son marry a goy (were she his mistress, Dona Frima says, it wouldn't matter), but as Senhor Arão told me in his letter, we should thank God that Nunho isn't in jail, that he got himself straightened out. That he is alive, in short. Nunho and Lina. A couple full of go, according to their friends. Which are legion, by the way.

Things have changed. Even here on Rua Voluntários: Benjamim's store and the New Jerusalem gave way to a big wholesale establishment—The Babylon Firm—and the place where Orígene's temple used to be now houses a car rental company.

And what about Doutor Alfredo? Already an old man, he walked out on his wife and went after Elvira, who was living in the country. They live together. He is devoting himself to farming and to studying Orígenes's diary, about which he intends to write a book. He has discovered profound spirituality in those pages. He stopped ransacking closets. *Nowdays I take orders from no one*, Elvira said in the only letter she has ever written to me. Every so often she pays a visit to Big Dog, who owns a farm some forty kilometers away; after serving out his sentence, he and Peep-Less began to raise small rodents for laboratory experiments. Elvira, of course, is still fond of him. Big Dog welcomes her at the door of his house; they chat for a few moments, all the while gazing intently at each other, and suddenly the two of them run to the bedroom, quickly take off their clothes, and make love while Peep-Less, vigilant, stands on guard, just in case Doutor Alfredo should turn up. As for Samir's brother—where is he? Where does he

fix his squint eye? Where does he fix his good eye? Which of
his two eyes might be shedding tears for his dead brother?

Speaking of tears, time goes by here in Porto Alegre. Months
and years. The months: windy Septembers, rainy Augusts,
Mays with their brief warm spells; hot Februaries, festive
Decembers, freezing-cold Julies; Januaries, Marches, Aprils,
Junes, Novembers. The years of President Medici and the years
of President Geisel ... Yes, years.

The newspapers never mentioned me again. They had far
more interesting news: the fuel crisis, inflation, the kidnapping
of the Uruguayans, the new political openness. One morning in
1973 I woke to the sound of the radio, which was just then
broadcasting a special news bulletin: the Yom Kippur War had
just broken out. Still groggy with sleep, I was startled: Now
he's going to run away again! But I soon came to my senses:
No, he won't, he's dead now, Benjamim is. I felt like crying—
since we're on the subject of tears—but I didn't cry, at least not
in that year, 1973. I cried before, but not in 1973.

Speaking of tears, I have nothing to complain about. I don't
complain about my life, there are others far worse. I don't
complain about the bar. It provides us with an income, with the
money to pay for my son's education. Two wonderful kids.
Tall, strong; good rowers, both of them. Last year I managed to
save enough money to make a dream come true; I gave them
a boat—a skiff—as a gift. Sometimes the three of us go rowing
together. On such occasions, I never cease to be amazed at the
swiftness with which the boys make the *Voluntários* glide among
the islands of the Guaíba River. Those islands are full of
mysterious things, I say to them. They laugh: Poppycock, Dad,
you're just a great storyteller.

I tell them stories, they don't believe me. They don't believe
in Orígenes, they don't believe in the whale, they don't
believe in the Captain, they don't believe in Benjamim, the friend
who wanted so badly to live in Jerusalem. I don't think they
believe in Jerusalem, either.

I myself have almost forgotten Jerusalem. The Golden City
has vanished from my thoughts, which in a way is a relief.
Unlike my friend Benjamim, I won't ever be afflicted with the
nostalgia for something I have never seen. One day—one

night—the walls and the towers, their stones undermined by heaven knows what invisible tunnels dug by heaven knows what pertinacious ants, the kind of ants that secrete heaven knows what acid capable of corroding rocks—the walls and the towers of my imagination silently collapsed and crumbled to dust, and this dust the wind then swept away. Of the Wailing Wall, only one single stone has remained, a stone that isn't as big as the others, but much smaller, about the size of those paving stones buried under the asphalt that now covers Rua Voluntários de Pátria.

Between the sky and the earth floats this stone, or so I imagine. And this makes me think: instead of our crazy attempt to take Benjamim to Jerusalem, we could have brought him a stone from the Wailing Wall. We could have asked somebody—Captain Andreas, the Reverend Jonathan, Father Francisco, Samir's folks, a pilgrim—in short, anyone, to send us a stone from the Wall. No matter how small. Wouldn't this stone, placed by Benjamim's head, have made him hear ancestral melodies? Wouldn't this stone have cured his cancer? This stone, or any other?

Silly ideas. A stone is a stone. Stones are not my line of business. And neither is storytelling—my sons are right. My business is to sell meat turnovers. And so I keep selling them. And eating them, which amounts to a form of protest: a ruinous yet irresistible form of protest. For they're so delicious, these meat turnovers. Rich, nourishing. As you see me eating one, sir, I can guess the question on your mind. Why do you open the meat turnover before eating it?

I don't know what to say in reply. A quirk of mine, perhaps. Perhaps I hope that one day, inside a meat turnover, no matter how dried up and cold, I'll find a beautiful silver watch with the emblem of the Hanseatic League. Of course, there's never any watch inside, just minced meat and hard-boiled egg.

But, my friend, think of this meat turnover. Think of the dough used to make it. Think of the flour. Think of the wheat—of how golden it grew in the sun of Rio Grande do Sul in order to yield the grains that were then ground into this flour.

Think of the meat. Think of the bull that was dying at

sunset. Think of the rump of beef, think of the knife cutting
into it, think of the morsels of meat. Try to hear the sizzling of
the frying pan, and in the background, an aria from the *Aida*
sung by a gentle female voice.

Think of the egg. Think of the hen laying this egg. Picture
this bird's unrestrained anguish, her purposeless longing.
Bring back to mind, if you have ever witnessed it, the birth of
the egg. And then, the egg being cooked. Imagine the water
at the boiling point, the white egg dancing at the whim of
turbulence. Imagine what's happening inside, the molecules of
the egg white and of the yolk massing together to form the
solid substance that characterizes a hard-boiled egg. Think of
all this, then tell me if this meat turnover needs a silver watch.
Tell me if my meat turnovers are overpriced, as rumor has it.
Tell me. But not now.

Now, if you'll excuse me, sir, I'm closing because it's late and
I'm tired. Tomorrow is another day. There'll be other stories.
Other journeys, for other volunteers.

TITLES OF THE AVAILABLE PRESS
in order of publication

THE CENTAUR IN THE GARDEN, a novel by Moacyr Scliar*
EL ANGEL'S LAST CONQUEST, a novel by Elvira Orphée
A STRANGE VIRUS OF UNKNOWN ORIGIN, a study by Dr. Jacques Leibowitch
THE TALES OF PATRICK MERLA, short stories by Patrick Merla
ELSEWHERE, a novel by Jonathan Strong*
THE AVAILABLE PRESS/PEN SHORT STORY COLLECTION
CAUGHT, a novel by Jane Schwartz*
THE ONE-MAN ARMY, a novel by Moacyr Scliar
THE CARNIVAL OF THE ANIMALS, short stories by Moacyr Scliar
LAST WORDS AND OTHER POEMS, poetry by Antler
O'CLOCK, short stories by Quim Monzó
MURDER BY REMOTE CONTROL, a novel in pictures
    by Janwillem van de Wetering and Paul Kirchner
VIC HOLYFIELD AND THE CLASS OF 1957, a novel by William Heyen*
AIR, a novel by Michael Upchurch
THE GODS OF RAQUEL, a novel by Moacyr Scliar*
SUTERISMS, pictures by David Suter
DOCTOR WOOREDDY'S PRESCRIPTION FOR ENDURING
    THE END OF THE WORLD, a novel by Colin Johnson
THE CHESTNUT RAIN, a poem by William Heyen
THE MAN IN THE MONKEY SUIT, a novel by Oswaldo França, Júnior
KIDDO, a novel by David Handler*
COD STREUTH, a novel by Bamber Gascoigne
LUNACY & CAPRICE, a novel by Henry Van Dyke
HE DIED WITH HIS EYES OPEN, a mystery by Derek Raymond
DUSTSHIP GLORY, a novel by Andreas Schroeder
FOR LOVE, ONLY FOR LOVE, a novel by Pasquale Festa Campanile
'BUCKINGHAM PALACE', DISTRICT SIX, a novel by Richard Rive
THE SONG OF THE FOREST, a novel by Colin Mackay
BE-BOP, RE-BOP, a novel by Xam Wilson Cartier
THE DEVIL'S HOME ON LEAVE, a mystery by Derek Raymond
THE BALLAD OF THE FALSE MESSIAH, a novel by Moacyr Scliar
little pictures, short stories by andrew ramer
THE IMMIGRANT: A Hamilton County Album, a play by Mark Harelik
HOW THE DEAD LIVE, a mystery by Derek Raymond
BOSS, a novel by David Handler
THE TUNNEL, a novel by Ernesto Sabato
THE FOREIGN STUDENT, a novel by Philippe Labro, translated by William R. Byron
ARLISS, a novel by Llyla Allen
THE CHINESE WESTERN: An Anthology of Short Fiction from Today's China,
    translated by Zhu Hong and Patricia van der Leun

*Available in a Ballantine Mass Market Edition.